With a startled look, Slocum pivoted and stared at the Apache's face. His left eye hung out from the socket. The big Apache strained and grunted and finally pulled himself up. He took his eye in his fingers and pushed the eye back in its socket. Slocum shuddered. Then the Apache walked toward the hut where Ibarruri lay.

"Jesus Christ!" breathed Cummings. "It's time we took off. For Christ's sake, stop him!"

"Not me," Slocum said.

"For God's sake, Snow!"

"They don't fight by our rules," Slocum said calmly. "I'm giving him three minutes alone with him. Then we're leaving."

"I've done my best to prevent acts of torture when I use Apache scouts—" Cummings began.

They heard a gasp and a moan inside the hut, then the sound of Ibarruri's body as it writhed and moved across the dirt floor in agony. Then came a long, stifled moan, then silence . . .

OTHER BOOKS BY JAKE LOGAN

JAKE LOGAN

SLOCUM'S COMMAND

BERKLEY BOOKS, NEW YORK

SLOCUM'S COMMAND

A Berkley Book / published by arrangement with
the author

PRINTING HISTORY
Berkley edition / November 1983

ISBN: 0-425-06532-4

A BERKLEY BOOK ® TM 757,375
Berkley Books are published by The Berkley Publishing Group,
200 Madison Avenue, New York, N.Y. 10016.
The name "BERKLEY" and the stylized "B" with design are trademarks
belonging to Berkley Publishing Corporation.

PRINTED IN THE UNITED STATES OF AMERICA

1

On a very rainy February night John Slocum broke out of the New Mexico Territorial Penitentiary. At a stagecoach station near Black Mesa he stole a saddled horse. Still dressed in the coarse gray prison attire, he pushed the horse all night. In the morning he ate mesquite beans, and all that day he ran the horse across southeastern Arizona and into Chiricahua territory, until the horse broke its foreleg between two flat rocks. Slocum did not like leaving the animal to suffer, but he did not have a gun, and even if he had, he certainly was not going to fire it and attract unwelcome attention from the Apaches.

It was late in the afternoon when he walked away from the horse. He moved south, toward Mexico and safety. Around six o'clock he heard some firing. He poked his head carefully over the crest of a ridge and saw a cavalry squad gone to ground and fighting desperately against an Apache ambush.

To Slocum, trained as a cavalry officer during the War, it was obvious that the unit had been neatly lured into a narrow defile. They were hopelessly outnumbered, and for once the Apaches had plenty of guns. Their firepower was massive; the horses were killed off first, then the soldiers were picked off one by one. When all movement had ceased on the field, the Apaches rose from behind their rocks and cautiously approached. One or two soldiers still stirred, but they were stabbed immediately.

As the Apaches bent for their ritual mutilation, Slocum heard a bugle call in the distance. A lookout posted on a ridge shouted a warning. The warriors seized whatever weapons they could find on the dead men and climbed the steep slopes where the heavily cumbered troopers could not follow.

Slocum looked at the dead men below. Looking up, he could see the scout come into view about two miles away. Then came the blue uniforms, two by two, riding at a fast trot. Even at this distance he could see the broad yellow stripes running down their trouser legs. He had fought those blue uniforms for four years and called them bluebellies, but now they were going to be a very big help to him.

He ran down the slope and found a body that was very much like his—tall, with broad shoulders and a slim waist. The man wore a captain's bars. He had been shot through the head and a little blood had trickled onto the right shoulder. His papers said he was Captain Paul Snow. Slocum tossed his prison clothes into a gully, put on Snow's outfit, picked up a sharp little rock, and gouged a bloody track across the right side of his head. That would explain his apparent unconsciousness. When the command arrived he opened his eyes and looked up with a dazed stare into the unblinking, harsh gaze of Colonel Israel Horton, Ninth U.S. Cavalry, out of Fort Grant.

"Jesus Christ, man, what happened?" Horton demanded sharply. He had cold gray eyes set in a ruddy face, and a brusque, impatient style which raised Slocum's hackles immediately. Slocum was sitting up against a rock watching the burial detachment busily at work. A corporal had put a bandage on his self-inflicted gash and wrapped gauze around it, and a quartermaster sergeant had given him a drink of whiskey. The liquor had an immediate effect on his empty stomach.

"They jumped us without warning," Slocum said, then cursed himself silently. Snow had been the highest ranking officer of the patrol, and the incident could not have occurred had he been alert. In any narrow defile he should have had his scouts out, but it was clear that the late Captain Snow had omitted this elementary precaution.

" 'Without warning,' " Horton repeated mockingly. "Do you realize you're responsible for the deaths of all these men, you incompetent son of a bitch?"

In these circumstances, a real army captain would flush angrily, and that is what Slocum did. It was not too hard; he had already conceived a very strong dislike for the abrasive colonel who stood in front of him, slapping his riding gloves against his thigh.

"What's your name?" Horton demanded brusquely.

"Captain Paul Snow, Third Cavalry."

"Sir!" Horton snapped.

"Yes, sir," Slocum said slowly.

"From Fort Grant?"

"Yes, sir."

Horton's gray eyes stared into Slocum's green ones. Slocum forced himself to play the role of a groggy officer who had narrowly escaped death, and although he had made a serious tactical error, was still too relieved to be alive to be thinking about his possible court-martial.

"Shit," Horton said. "I'm not going to send you back with an escort. I can't spare anyone to be a nursemaid to some incompetent fool. You'll come with us, and when I give you an order, try to carry it out without falling over your feet. Think you can do that much?"

Some of the officers standing around tittered, others stayed silent. Slocum could see that Horton had his favorites—those who laughed at his remarks. There were others who did not care for him. Slocum noticed a heavy-set captain in his late forties with a full face and a graying mustache, whose eyebrows were raised in faint contempt at Horton's bandying of a man who had, after all, just been through a rough experience. His name, Slocum would later learn, was William Cummings.

2

The command crossed into Mexico at dusk and made camp by the Rio San Gregorio. They were chasing a large band of hostile Apaches who had burned and tortured their way across southern Arizona.

At three in the morning, while Slocum was sleeping the sleep of pure exhaustion, several shots were fired into the horse lines.

Captain Cummings whipped off his blanket and came on the run. Slocum followed somewhat more slowly. He had not been given any duties and he realized that with an experienced officer like Cummings around there was nothing to do. After Cummings had stopped the sentries from wasting any more ammunition, he went back to his blanket and pulled off his boots once more. He was annoyed and he made no bones about it to Slocum.

While he complained in a good-humored fashion, he rubbed his back. A Confederate cavalryman had slashed him with a saber in the Valley. He thought wryly how he used to sleep on the damp earth and leap up eagerly at reveille. When he had gotten all settled again in the blanket a rough hand shook him awake. There was no sign of light in the east. It was Rigby, the colonel's orderly.

"Captain, the colonel wants you right away, he says. He says to bring the new fellow." Cummings stared up at

5

the dark mass above him. Rigby was devoted to the colonel, who in turn took good care to see that the man's minor transgressions were not punished. Cummings did not like Rigby referring to Slocum as the new fellow, but it was too early to start an argument.

Cummings shook Slocum awake. As they pulled on their boots, Cummings silently cursed this fool expedition, whoever had shot into his horses, and the hundreds of miles they would be covering in a hostile country.

Slocum followed Cummings toward the yellow glow of the kerosene lamp hanging in the colonel's tent. Lieutenant Palmer, the colonel's nephew, only a few months out of West Point, sat sprawled in a camp chair smoking a cigar. In one hand he held a bottle of expensive bourbon—nothing but the best, Slocum noted, in *this* outfit—and in his other hand he held a glass which he was busily engaged in filling. He grunted in Cummings's direction but did not offer him a drink. He paid no attention to Slocum, who wasted no energy getting annoyed at the man's poor manners. Slocum wanted to size everyone up carefully before he made any moves.

Sitting cross-legged on the ground next to the lieutenant was Eskiminzin, a Mescalero Apache scout. Eskiminzin liked Cummings; he had taught Apache to the graying captain. His teeth flashed in his wide dark brown face. Across the knees of his dirty white breeches lay the Winchester carbine that would be his after the expedition. His fat brown fingers caressed the stock, back and forth, back and forth, as if he were polishing it.

On a small folding table under the hanging lantern lay a map of Chihuahua.

"Sit down," Horton said curtly. He did not look up. His superbly booted and spurred foot shoved a stool across. Cummings sat down. Slocum stood behind him and noticed that Cummings was looking at the famous curly black head as it bent over the map. Horton's hair was beginning to thin at the crown, and several white hairs had appeared at the temples. Cummings crossed his legs, grinned up at Slocum, winked, and lit his own cigar—a cheap one, Slocum observed with some amusement.

In a corner leaned the colonel's personal guidon, a small yellow forked flag. Across the bottom were the words SEVEN PINES.

Cummings leaned back and beckoned Slocum to bend down. "That's where he got his brigadier star," he whispered.

Slocum permitted himself a wide smile. He had been a very young lieutenant at that battle, very scared, and on the other side.

The guidon had fluttered and snapped behind Horton in the Sioux country along the Powder River; it had plunged after him, set into Rigby's stirrup, in a dawn charge against a Cheyenne encampment in eastern Colorado. The three bullet holes in it, Horton was positive, had always brought him luck. When Horton looked up suddenly from the map he caught Cummings's dry, derisive stare and flushed angrily. Eskiminzin's black eyes glittered as he felt the sudden tension between the two officers. Then he dropped his gaze back to the walnut stock and went on stroking it.

Horton looked down at the map. "Here we are," he said briskly. His well manicured finger pointed to the foot of a small range. "We have a hundred and fifty miles to go before we get down in the Sierra Madre where what's-his-name here says they hole up. Now the question is, are those Apaches who fired into the horse lines tonight from the same bands down in the Sierra? D'you think they'll ride down and tell 'em we're coming? What d'you think, Cummings?"

Cummings had more experience than the colonel in the Southwest and everyone knew it. As much as Horton hated to ask, he had to.

Cummings removed his cigar from his mouth and looked at the end of it. "First of all," he said, "that wasn't Apaches firing into us. They—"

"How do you know?" Lieutenant Palmer demanded.

Young puppy, Cummings thought. The young man had come out from the Point a few months before at Horton's request; he was the colonel's nephew, and Horton believed in taking care of his own.

"Them was Meskins," Eskiminzin said suddenly. His coarse black hair was held in place by a narrow red band above his forehead. "Them Chiricahuas we're chasin'—why, they don't got ammunition to waste like that. They got to rob their ammunition. They get it from the miners, they get it from Meskin traders—they don' go wastin' it. They good shots." He grinned.

"All right," Horton said, satisfied. Next he wanted to know what route they should take in order to avoid running into hostile Apaches.

Eskiminzin could not read maps. He picked out a carbine cartridge from his worn bandolier. Leaning forward, his bandolier creaking, he began to draw in the dirt. "We go 'long this here canyon, mebbe two days, mebbe three . . ."

Slocum watched as the colonel listened attentively, drawing lines on the map, questioning. Slocum turned his gaze upon Cummings, who was drawing upon the stub of his cigar and staring at Horton's spurs. They had been scrubbed with brass polish with such fierce devotion by Rigby, the orderly, that the lantern reproduced itself all over the spurs in myriad tiny sunbursts. With a small, amused smile Cummings leaned forward and stubbed out his cigar, aware, Slocum was sure, of Rigby's disapproving glance at his own tarnished spurs.

After the meeting, back under his blanket, Cummings laced his arms beneath his head and stared up into the cloudless night sky.

Slocum liked the man. "Penny for your thoughts, Captain," he said.

"I bet you know what I'm thinking," Cummings replied with a sigh. "But I'll tell you anyway. Will he get away with it this time? I bet he will. His luck has never run out. He provoked this particular uprising by shooting their medicine man. Did you know that?"

"No, I didn't," Slocum replied, somewhat disturbed.

"That's funny," Cummings observed. "Thought the whole goddamn cavalry knew about it." He turned his head to stare at Slocum, who cursed under his breath. A man in prison didn't exactly get to read the local papers as soon as they placed on sale.

Slocum shrugged. "Too busy," he said. "Was in charge of the pack trains—no mules, packers drunk . . ." He shrugged.

Cummings laughed. "They sure work damn well better than the old wagon trains," he said. "Good thing Crook developed 'em. Where was I? Yeah." He continued, his suspicions allayed. "Well, the whole damn thing was predictable. The Apaches burned ranch houses and roasted propectors all over southern Arizona. So everyone demands that the savages must be punished. And who gets sent out by Sheridan in Omaha? Horton. *That's* predictable.

"Yes," Cummings went on, staring up at the Big Dipper, which seemed to be caught between the branches of an oak tree. "Horton shot old Nachodise in the back when the old man was crawling away into the chaparral. He knew damn well that would provoke an uprising, with all the water in the lower Gila being taken out by miners up river and none of it getting down to the Apaches on their corn lands lower down. So some Apaches who were starving shot a few cattle, and next the ranchers shot any Apaches they came across—and so on and so on. You know that old saying about laurels being scarce along Indian trails? You know damn well how hard it is to get any notice in

Washington—much less a goddamn promotion—fighting Indians. A skirmish here, a skirmish there, two men dead, one man wounded—who gives a damn? I think Horton's looking for some spectacular action. But why go down two hundred miles into Mexico after Apaches? He knows damn well the regulations don't allow us to go more than fifty miles into Mexico, and that only on a hot trail. The Mexicans hate us. They don't want us even going one mile into their country.''

"You're sure it was Mexicans out there tonight?" Slocum asked.

Cummings looked at him. "Snow," he said, "if Eskiminzin says it was Mexicans, it was Mexicans. Not a single Mexican wants us here, not even to kill Apaches. Down in Hermosillo they pay fifty pesos for Apache scalps. Well, if we turn back after fifty miles we'll be nowhere near the Sierra—and back we go again, with nothing to show for it but some lame horses, some bad cases of sunstroke, a couple men bitten by scorpions, maybe a couple rattlesnake bites, one or two men picked off along the way by Mexicans or Apaches, a few horses stolen, and a few damn fools deserting. What I can't understand is why he provoked the uprising, if this is the way it will end.''

"Maybe we'll fight Apaches," Slocum offered. Slocum had no objection to the journey, as long as he was with this cavalry patrol. At least he would be protected by the group and decently fed until the time came for him, too, to desert in friendly country. He was beginning to like Cummings's air of amused, dry cynicism.

They heard footsteps approaching. It was Lieutenant Palmer, Horton's nephew. "I heard that, Snow," he said. "I wouldn't mind fighting those red devils myself."

Slocum shook his head. He wasn't as eager as the younger man; he had lost several good friends who had spent their last hours spread-eagled naked under the pitiless, brilliant, scorching sun while the Apache women tortured them.

"Stop talking like an editor on one of those papers back East," Cummings told Palmer contemptuously. "You know how Apaches move?" he went on. "Suppose you're trailing one and he comes to desert country. It's hilly, hot, no water in sight. You have one canteen of water. He has none. He kills his horse—or one that belongs to you, if he's afoot. He fills its guts with water, wraps the guts around and around himself. Then he runs all day. I said *runs*. He will run seventy-five miles a day. If your horse does forty in the heat, it's a miracle. And that's supposing you find water. If there's no water in the desert, be smart. Just turn around and go home."

Palmer began to speak, but Cummings wouldn't give him the chance.

"Know how they train the youngsters?" the captain went on. "When the boy's about ten, his father takes him out to the desert and gives him a mouthful of water. He tells the kid not to swallow it, just keep it in his mouth. Then he points to a mountain ten miles away. There's a certain plant that grows only on the top. The kid has to run across the desert—and it's when the sun is right overhead, when all the sensible animals are panting under the bushes—and the kid has to run to the mountain, bring back the plant, and then spit out the water he was holding in his mouth. *All* of it.

"And yet fighting Apaches is the easiest part of campaigning. Know what the hardest part is?"

Slocum waited, curious. He knew that the average white soldier would look at a couple of Apaches from thirty feet away, turn aside for a moment, and then turn back. The Apaches would have vanished as completely as a pair of crested mountain quail.

"Finding 'em," Cummings said, as Slocum had expected.

3

Long before dawn the Apache stripped himself naked and rubbed clay from the riverbed all over himself. Next he tied a bunch of sacaton grass to his head. Two hours later, the clay had dried till it was the same color as the Chihuahuan soil. He lay on a small rise fifty yards from the camp and twenty feet from the river. His gray, rough-caked body blended perfectly with the soil. No part of his body moved except his hard black eyes. His gray hand rested on a lance whose blade was formed from an officer's sword on which the date 1837 was still faintly visible. Both shaft and blade were smeared with clay also. Not even the Mexicans who had fired into the camp had seen the Apache, though they passed within three feet of him.

Several troopers were washing their horses in the river while two guards stood idly by, yawning and sniffing the coffee that was being heated up by the cooks. But the Apaches knew that sooner or later someone would get careless and wander too close to him. He did not mind waiting.

Cummings and Slocum were bathing upriver from the horses. Then they shaved, using a round mirror that Cummings hung from a broken cottonwood branch. Eskiminzin sat nearby on a log, eating his bacon and beans. His eyes

13

moved constantly; he had great contempt for the eyesight and the alertness of the white sentries.

"Where are the Apaches?" demanded Cummings. "Where is *any* hostile Indian? When I rode over from Texas they said I was sure to be shot at on the Brazos. Then they said I was certain to be attacked on the Concho; then it was killed and scalped at Saddle Gap. Burned alive in Olympia Canyon, they said. Killed all over again in Apache Pass and my scalp taken for a drum. I must admit I saw a cactus once that looked like an Apache . . ."

Slocum had seen the slightest movement in the caked clay across the river. He turned to the scout, who had not noticed it. When the Apache looked up, Slocum gave a tiny inclination of his head toward the motionless mass across the river. Eskiminzin looked, then placed his plate carefully on the ground; he did not want to spill anything. He brought his carbine around casually, as if to examine it. Then he brought it up swiftly to his shoulder and fired so fast that Cummings fell backward, thinking the man had suddenly gone amok. But Eskiminzin's calm grin reassured him. Thirty feet away, the sun-baked lump of clay quivered, then fell silent.

"Them Chiricahuas bad pipple," Eskiminzin said cheerfully, and ejected the empty cartridge. The brass case spun end over end, glinting in the rising sun, and finally rolled to a stop. He picked it up and stowed it away carefully. He would either trade it later or reload it himself, when he had the proper tools.

The dry ground quickly soaked up the blood trickling down the caked clay. "They steal hosses right offa the fort," Eskiminzin went on. "They take 'em back to our reservation, make the officers think we Mescaleros did the stealin'." He frowned, shoved another cartridge into the carbine, and pumped a new one into the chamber as the sentries came running up to look at the dead Apache.

"They try to git us into trouble so's we'll join 'em." He

grinned and rubbed a tremendous brown hand over his head. With the spread of white teeth in his lower jaw he looked to Slocum like a fat, bronzed shark. Around his neck he wore a necklace of heavy turquoise beads alternating with silver squash blossoms. Eskiminzin looked at Slocum with new respect. He thought that this new white officer had eyesight as good as an Apache's.

"My father, he tol' 'em, don' take them Army hosses! My father, he was learnin' how to farm. He knew there was no more raidin' 'n' takin' prisoners—all over. They called 'im out in the yard an' lanced 'im. It was hard to kill my pop. I counted thirty lance holes in him. I come home two days later, else things woulda been diff'rent."

He grinned again and spread out all his fingers to their fullest extent. One of his hands could easily cover Slocum's and leave an inch more all around.

"They fine, strong men. Well, they got plenty hosses, plenty guns. They don' hunt no more. They jus' steal, steal, steal all the time. They bad pipple. They jus' kill ev'rybody they find in the mountains. Bad pipple." He shook his head in dismay. "Some day I ketch them Chiricahuas who kilt my pop," he finished happily. "Then his spirit will rest. His spirit comes to me in dreams an' asks me, how long? I say soon, Pop."

Two of the soldiers had gone to get shovels. "You don' have to do nothin'," he said disapprovingly. "Them *zapilotes* will do it." High above them five black birds were drifting down.

"He's right," Cummings told the sentries. "Leave him alone." He looked a bit sick.

"What's the matter?" Slocum asked the captain. "You wanted a hostile Apache, didn't you?"

"Yes," Cummings said, "and I'll never ask for another."

* * *

On the march, Slocum caught the hard glare Lieutenant Palmer was sending toward Cummings. The intensity of the hatred surprised him.

"Kid doesn't like you much," he muttered into Cummings's ear, leaning over from his saddle. High up in the blue sky some hawks were spiraling. The wind from the mountain slopes of the Sierra Madre blew across the flats.

Cummings shrugged and laughed, a rueful, half bitter, half amused laugh. "Like so many important things, it all began with such an insignificant thing. . . ." His eyes were on the horizon in the distance, but Slocum could tell he was looking back at the insignificant event.

"Well," Cummings said at last, "it began during the War. Some ferry landing on a goddamn creek in Virginia. A reporter I knew had just put some rebel papers aboard the mail boat. Rebel papers were scarce up north in those days, and I suppose his editor wanted them very much.

"Horton rode up to me; I'd never seen him before. He was a captain and I was a brand new second lieutenant, fresh out of the Point, like that asinine young Palmer there. Horton said to me, pretty snappy, 'General McLean wants those papers that reporter just put aboard the mail boat, mister!'

"I flared up immediately, even though he was wearing those captain's bars. It was his tone I couldn't stand: as if I were a stupid five-year-old.

" 'Get 'em yourself,' I told him. I had just come from battle, and Horton looked so neat, in a freshly pressed uniform, as if he had just stepped out of the War Department office. I thought he was a desk officer, you see. I had no idea he was a very brave and very smart field officer and had won those captain's bars, not through seniority, but for leading a cavalry charge right through a reb detachment. He was looking for prisoners to get information from, and he brought his men back without a scratch. Had his horse killed, grabbed a reb horse, and rode it back with five prisoners, one a colonel. He deserved that captaincy.

"So I was insulting to him. He said, 'You're under arrest, sir! Get your horse and follow me!'

"He rode north, not even looking behind to see if I was following. I was an officer and so was he, and he was so sure that I would obey a direct order that he never looked around. So I rode south, and by the time he realized that I wasn't there, several field pieces with all their horses and baggage had blocked the landing. He knew that further pursuit over such a petty incident would make him a laughingstock, so he just watched me ride away.

"Three days later he caught up with me outside a courthouse at Warrenton. I was sitting with several other young officers on a sofa we had taken from inside the courthouse. We were eating fried chicken and corn bread, our first decent meal in a week, and he rode up. He recognized me immediately.

"He started yelling at me for not obeying him. Everyone stopped eating except me. I gnawed on a drumstick and listened to that tirade. Maybe he was exhausted, maybe things had gone badly—but he was almost hysterical. Over nothing—*nothing*, mind you. Finally he ran down and stood there panting.

"I said, 'You are making an exhibition out of yourself for nothing. You are behaving like a drummer boy, not an officer. Take off your shoulder bars and go back to school again.'

"Everyone laughed. Horton flushed red, came closer, and stared at me. I must admit that a little chill went through me. He has gray eyes, and they looked like chips of ice. I knew that I had overstepped the bounds of wisdom with my remarks. But I said, 'Take a good look, Captain.' And he did. He remembered me—oh, he remembered me very well. I have no doubt that he's responsible for blocking my promotion."

Cumming sighed, then said cheerfully, "No use crying over spilt milk, eh?" He reached across and slapped Slocum on his shoulder. "Life should teach us to enjoy every moment, not to dwell on what cannot be helped. So let's enjoy this enchanting desert!"

Slocum liked him. He had been planning to quietly depart with the cavalry horse he was riding in a day or so, but he was becoming intrigued with the relations between Horton and Cummings. And that arrogant young lieutenant, Palmer, Horton's nephew, deserved to be taken down a peg or two. It would be more interesting to hang around for a while yet. He could always desert on the way back and leave with an even better horse than the one he was riding. Horton's favorite mount, Congaree, a big bay, would command a high price if offered to a rich Mexican rancher. Slocum had begun to dislike the colonel thoroughly. It would be a pleasure to steal Congaree and dispose of him in Mexico. Afterwards, if Horton ever ran across Slocum and recognized him as the man who had stolen Congaree, there would be no way he could assemble the evidence or see it through to an indictment, if the theft happened in Mexico.

Slocum grinned. This had the elements he loved: an unpleasant fellow suffering major discomfiture and a crime so neatly committed that prosecution was impossible.

Cummings and Slocum rode along in companionable silence. The floor of the desert flat shimmered and shook in the heat haze. Everything lost color and seemed to drain away into various shades of washed-out gray. As they rode into a canyon, Cummings made sure that the scouts were ranging ahead. The canyon walls turned to a quivering bronze and tiny brown lizards flicked across the trail, stopped short to observe the command, then flicked themselves away into invisibility.

Cummings said, "Ever read about Sir John Franklin?"

Slocum took a sip from his canteen, rinsed his mouth,

and let the warm water trickle slowly down his throat. He
shook his head. A man who spent his life in the West had
very little time for reading. It took enough energy just to
eat and to stay alive. Once in a winter line camp in
northern Colorado, when he was snowed in for four months,
he had read everything he could get his hands on, but the
tastes of the cowpunchers who had inhabited that cabin
leaned toward the *Police Gazette* and some back issues of
the *Cattlemen's Journal*. He shook his head.

"Ah, well," Cummings said wistfully. "He went up to
the Arctic Ocean looking for some vanished expedition or
other. Or he was on one—I forget. I only read it to feel
cool, anyway. Every time I read about fishing through a
hole in the ice it gave me enough energy to pass another
day in the goddamned Arizona desert." He waved away
the little green flies that kept stinging him through his sweat.
"If you want, I'll lend you my copy."

"No, thanks," Slocum said dryly.

"Of course you wouldn't want it," Cummings said with
a wide grin. "A man named Snow would feel cool all the
time."

They watched as Eskiminzin and Lieutenant Palmer rode
almost to the top of a ridge ahead. They dismounted and
crawled to the top. Slocum looked inquiringly at Cummings.

Cummings shrugged. "Colonel wants the kid to get
experience," he he said sourly. "If you ask me, that
young fool is never going to learn anything. He's a mite
too arrogant, too sure of himself. And with his uncle to
fortify his smug assurance . . ." He shrugged again.

Palmer started to get up. Eskiminzin put a hand on his
shoulder and pushed him down. Palmer was annoyed. He
shook the Apache's hand off and started to rise again.
Eskiminzin forced him flat easily with his huge hand.
Cummings grinned and looked at Slocum, who had caught
the little byplay. Palmer looked through the field glasses
once again, obviously instructed to do so by the scout.

Impatiently he turned to the Apache and started to give him an argument.

Slocum began to grin. He had been through that once before, long ago, with a Crow scout in Montana. He had been out hunting grizzly as a respite from gold prospecting, and he had done the same thing. He had searched the whole valley and ridge for bear sign and, not seeing any, had been about to stand up. The Crow had pressed him flat and pointed to a big brown mass which Slocum, with field glasses, had thought was a dried bough from a fallen oak. But it was a grizzly, perfectly still and staring at him. From then on, Slocum would rather trust the sharp eyes of an Indian than any pair of glasses, no matter how good.

By the time Cummings and Slocum had reached the ridge Palmer had picked up in his glasses to see what Eskiminzin had seen without them. Thirty Mexican horsemen were cantering toward the command.

Eskiminzin said to himself in Apache, "That's a beautiful horse!"

Slocum replied in the same language that it was, indeed, a beautiful horse. Palmer listened with envy.

The Apache looked at Slocum in delighted astonishment. He did not know that Slocum had once spent six months living with some Chiricahua while he recovered from a bad knife wound—and that it was either learn Apache or say nothing.

The strange riders neared. The commander of the detachment was riding a superb Arabian, its skin as black as oiled silk. They had ridden hard for two days to catch up, and they looked it.

Colonel Horton moved to the vanguard and rode ahead to meet them. Cummings gave quiet orders to stand at ease but to be ready for a quick dismount, and to take firing positions flat on their bellies when he gave the word to dismount.

The Mexicans reined in and brought their rifles around

to the ready. Horton turned to Cummings. "You speak Spanish, don't you? You do the talking. But don't say anything stupid."

Slocum saw Cummings flush at the unprovoked insult. Palmer tittered, and so did Horton's sycophants among the officers.

Cummings did the only thing he could have done: he did not respond.

"Snow," Horton said crisply.

"Sir?" Slocum asked.

"You speak Spanish, don't you?"

"Yes, sir."

"Come along. I need someone else, who can function as a check upon some impetuous translating."

Slocum nodded, his face impassive. He felt sorry for Cummings, who had to stand still for this kind of treatment. Slocum was determined that if any of it ever came his way he'd not stand for it.

The three men rode out. Horton held his hand palm out as a peace sign. Everyone on the frontier used that gesture, which had originated with the Indians, to show that their hands did not carry a weapon.

The Mexicans were restless as they stared at Eskiminzin. They hated and feared Apaches, and here was one who was armed with a good carbine and riding with the hated Americans. It was almost too much to bear. They stared at the command, which was so much better armed and equipped than they were.

The commander introduced himself as Don Gabriel Herrera Fonseca y Sandoval. The name conveyed aristocracy and noble lineage. His gold epaulets were the size of small saucers. His soldiers wore dirty peon clothes, and had obviously been conscripted from the neighborhood as a sort of reluctant militia.

As soon as Cummings had finished translating the polite introductory remarks, while the two commanders were taking a careful look at each other's men and equipment, Cummings leaned over and whispered to Slocum. "Look at 'em! They get issued three cartridges each for the march. Standard Mexican Army practice. If one of 'em is missing at inspection, the man could be executed. Rebels pay damn well for cartridges. Powder brings good money, too. Officers'll pry off the bullet to see if the powder's been extracted. But before a battle they issue plenty of cartridges. Run your eyes over 'em to see if you can spot any full bandoliers."

Slocum had already looked. The bandoliers were full, and men who were without bandoliers had their pockets bulging with cartridges.

Horton was aware of the risk. He did not like their position in this narrow valley, where they were exposed to fire from above should another Mexican detachment, having escaped his scouts' observation, be approaching at that moment for an attack.

Cummings, a cunning old strategist, knew what was on Horton's mind. He edged his horse close and casually mentioned that the scouts were out and vigilant. Horton grunted grudgingly.

"You are aware of the treaty?" Don Gabriel demanded. He stared with distaste at Eskiminzin. The Mexicans had been fighting Apaches over two hundred years longer than the Americans, and several times had been forced to abandon profitable gold and silver mines or good ranches because of incessant, merciless Apache raids.

"Of course," Horton said calmly. The statement surprised Don Gabriel. He had expected a denial. Slocum suppressed a grin just as he saw a woman ride out from the darkened end of the canyon.

Slocum had seen a good many attractive women in his time, but this one was something special. She had a faint olive complexion mixed with rose. Her long, glossy black hair hung in two long braids, one over each shoulder. Her lips were pale rose and her eyes were jet black. She was unusually tall for an Indian woman and fuller breasted than most of them. Her long legs were clad in a long black divided skirt made of wool. She wore an embroidered blouse made of cotton, and she rode astride. Her wide brimmed sombrero hung down her back by its chin strap. Her right hand, closed into a fist, was placed on her hip. Slocum judged her to be a *mestiza*, half Spanish, half Indian. Which tribe he could not guess, although for a moment he was tempted, because of her height, to guess that she was Blackfoot. She rode easily and with obvious competence, as though she'd been born to the saddle.

An annoyed expression flitted across Don Gabriel's face. Both Slocum and Cummings caught it. Cummings whispered, "I bet he thinks a woman's place is in the home and nowhere else."

Slocum responded, "And in the home it's the bed."

Cummings laughed. Horton pulled his gaze away from the woman, gave the two officers a swift angered look, then turned back.

Don Gabriel made a flicking gesture with his hand at her, telling her very clearly in sign language to get the hell out. She coolly disregarded him and stared at the American officers with unabashed interest. To prove that she had no intention of leaving she dismounted in one swift, liquid movement. As one leg went high up to clear the saddle horn Slocum, with a startled look, realized that she was naked under the skirt. She had made the move so that she was facing him. It was clear to Slocum that she had singled him out for this display.

She stood now, legs wide apart, hands on her hips, holding the reins of her horse. Don Gabriel, evidently realizing that any further attempt to make her leave would only be embarrassing to him and would only result in a scene, pretended that she did not exist.

"Yes," Horton said, "I am aware of the treaty."

"Well, then, Colonel?"

She had folded her arms under her breasts so that they were pushed up under her blouse. Again Slocum could see that she wore nothing underneath.

"And the fifty-mile rule?" The soldiers behind Don Gabriel had dispersed themselves in the shade of the low bushes nearby and tilted their wide-brimmed, high-crowned sombreros over their faces. They looked exhausted. They did not look like men planning a sudden, treacherous attack. Some of them sat cross-legged, smoking *cigarillos,* fanning themselves with their sombreros, staring at Eskiminzin and talking quietly. One man grinned when he saw Eskiminzin looking at him. The Mexican drew his forefinger across his throat. Slocum looked quickly at the Chiricahua, who muttered quietly. Slocum chuckled and translated for Cummings.

"He called him a coyote," Slocum said. "The literal meaning is 'He who customarily howls at dawn.' "

"But we are not fifty miles into Mexico at all," Horton said politely. He ran his knuckle slowly back and forth along the bottom edge of his neat mustache.

"Dirty liar," Cummings whispered. Slocum forced himself not to laugh. He admired Horton's diplomatic aplomb.

Don Gabriel shrugged and snapped his fingers. A ragged *mestizo* orderly presented a map. "Unroll it, idiot!" snapped the commander. The *mestizo* unrolled it and held it open in front of himself.

"Put it on the ground!" Don Gabriel raged. "I don't want to smell you." The soldier, impassive, placed it on the ground, weighted the corners with stones, and withdrew.

"I did not tell you to leave, idiot. Give me a stick!"

Still impassive, the man found a dead branch nearby and handed it to his commander.

"You are here, sir," he said gravely and courteously to Horton.

"I love their manners," Cummings said to Slocum.

"Exquisite politeness while they plot to cut your throat. If a man's got to die, at least let it be with good manners."

Slocum repressed a smile. He was busy watching Don Gabriel, the woman, and Colonel Horton. It was in such infinite attention to the details of facial expressions and tiny gestures that Slocum learned a great deal about people's intentions. And he was doubly in enemy country: first, posing as an army officer, and secondly, in a country where the local commander would dearly like to kill them all. Not to mention what the Apaches would do to him or any of them if they caught one soldier alone.

"You are here, sir," Don Gabriel repeated. To make his point clear, he jabbed the end of the branch at a valley Slocum recognized as being the one where they all stood. The teamsters had taken the packs off the mules, and the animals were rolling on their backs in ecstasy. Slocum looked at the woman. She had reached up a brown hand and gripped the saddle horn while she stared at Slocum. When she knew that Slocum's gaze had shifted to her, she gently and very slowly ran her closed palm up and down the horn, a tiny smile clinging to the corners of her rosy lips.

Slocum pursed his lips. There was no doubt about the sexual implications of that bit of silent language. No one else had noticed it; they were all staring at the map on the ground.

"Perhaps you are not aware of how far you have strayed over the fifty-mile boundary. After all, there are no road signs in Mexico."

Don Gabriel chuckled. Horton's face was immobile as granite.

Don Gabriel continued. He wished to avoid an incident, but it was his duty to persuade these Americans to go back. He hated them; he had the feeling that the leader of a well armed and well trained unit such as this one would not listen to him. Still, he had to try.

"You are over ninety miles inside Mexico, Colonel. The maps are not very good," he told Horton.

He was making it easy for the Americans to withdraw gracefully by agreeing with him and laying all the blame on defective maps.

He was surprised when Horton said he understood how it was very likely that Don Gabriel, in his turn, had made a natural error. It was true that Horton's troops had been in Mexico for three days. But, since they were not moving straight south into the country, but parallel to the border, they were only thirty miles from the United States.

Cummings stared at Horton.

"Translate," Horton said.

"That's a pretty large statement, sir. I—"

"You'll translate it the way I told it or I'll get someone who's not scared," Horton said indifferently, as if Cummings's objection carried as little weight as a mosquito bite.

Cummings flushed, but he turned to the Mexican and translated. The Mexican smiled, seeing the obvious hostility between the two American officers.

He said, "I think it would be better for you to go back now. Even if you are only thirty miles inside, as you claim."

There was the tiniest pause after the word "inside," and Slocum hid a smile at the very clear implication that Horton was a crude liar.

Don Gabriel added smoothly, "There are rebel troops, as you may or may not know, who have never heard of the treaty. They will not know that you have a right to be fifty miles inside Mexico. They will not realize that you are—as you say—only thirty miles from the border. To go on would not be wise. I could not guarantee their restraint if they should run across you. It is clear, is it not, that by definition rebels would pay no attention to any attempt on my part to persuade them to refrain from rash behavior?"

"What the hell is this son of a bitch trying to say?" demanded Horton.

At the words "son of a bitch" Don Gabriel stiffened. Slocum was pretty sure that the Mexican did not understand English, but every Mexican along the border who had met any Americans knew very well what that phrase meant.

"He means it wouldn't be safe for us to go on," Cummings said briefly. His voice showed scorn for the undiplomatic language of his commanding officer. Slocum agreed silently with Cummings's judgment. There was no point making a bad situation worse. And one thing was sure—it was going to get worse; there was no question about it.

"Well, pig shit!" Horton exploded. "Ask him right out if it wouldn't be safe for us to go on."

Cummings turned and translated, leaving out "pig shit."

"Yes, *safe*," Don Gabriel said, as he prepared to mount. "Very safe. Only a little shooting, maybe, by the rebel troops. Quite safe. But it would be better to go back."

Clever fellow, Slocum thought. The Mexican would be attacking soon. But the blame would be placed on the rebels both by him and by Horton if there should be any incidents. Don Gabriel's commanders would be pleased, since the attack would be seen as coming from rebels not under government authority; Don Gabriel would be commended and perhaps get a promotion, for he had made a formal complaint to the American commander about his presence in Mexico. The only thing that might go wrong would be that quite a few people would be dead by morning.

It would be a good time for Slocum to leave the command. The fight that would be taking place soon was not of his making. Slocum had ridden along for mutual protection, and there was no reason for him to hang around any more. There was no question of honor involved here; he had not sworn loyalty to this army, and he'd be damned if he ever would.

Still, he liked Cummings, and he was curious as to what Don Gabriel had up his sleeve. And Slocum wanted to see that beautiful girl and find out what she looked like naked. To do that, he would just have to go along with the command. For it was obvious that she would be with Don Gabriel—and Don Gabriel was planning, like a bull terrier, to sink his teeth into the Americans and hang on.

So Slocum would stick around.

Horton mounted. For a moment the two officers stared at each other. One of Horton's gloved hands rested low on his right hip. The fingers were spread out on his upper thigh. Then the hand shifted to his pistol butt and balanced there. Three paces to the rear, Rigby, the colonel's orderly, by twisting his ugly, scarred red neck, could catch sight of the colonel's face. He recognized the thoughtful, smiling expression and the slow, controlled breathing that went with it. It was the face of a skilled commander about to enter into battle.

Rigby gripped the guidon staff and seated it more firmly in his stirrup. He saw Cummings's angry, disturbed face, and felt nothing but contempt. Rigby missed the hot excitement of the battle flags, which, years ago, massed like a jammed flower garden floating above the blue regiments, had followed Horton's new yellow guidon as he pounded down a dusty lane somewhere in Virginia.

Horton turned to Cummings and said almost contemptuously, "Forward."

As Cummings swung into his saddle and repeated the order the *mestizo* rolled up the map and the bugler sounded "Mount!" The Americans trotted past Don Gabriel. He did not move as the dust swirled about him. He was counting the men as the command moved deeper into Mexico.

Slocum rode easy, with a small smile on his face. This promised to be intriguing.

4

"You see," Cummings said, "I have understood Horton
from the beginning."

He lit a pipe and happily sipped at his bourbon, staring
at the campfire. "I understand the Young Napoleon. Did
you know that's what they used to call him?"

Slocum leaned back and crossed legs at the ankle. He
clasped his hands behind his head. They were in a tent just
below the crest of a small hill which faced south. A full
moon as big and yellow as a pumpkin had just slid up over
the ridge ahead of them. Cummings was silent. He took
the pipe out of his mouth and pointed it at the moon.

"My little girl wanted to know if we had the same moon
down here as she was used to seeing back in Illinois. I told
her no, it wasn't so pretty. But it *is* prettier down
here, isn't it? Must be something to do with the higher
altitude. . . ." He was obviously thinking of his wife and
daughter, Slocum saw, and probably feeling depressed
because he was sure he would never get the promotion
that could make his years as a retired officer comfortable.
And it was Horton who had seen to that.

Cummings went on, filling his pipe with tobacco from a
worn leather pouch. "Horton did his best to get some
reporters along on this expedition. He pulled wires left and
right, tried to get artists from *Harper's*, wrote letters by

29

the score. And one reason he's as grouchy as a grizzly who's caught his balls in a bear trap is that not a one showed up. They were probably busy elsewhere and couldn't make it in time, even though Horton was promising 'em all a nice, colorful little war. Another reason is that there's a few people in the War Department who're mighty jealous of the Young Napoleon, and quite possibly saw to it that the editors received hints not to be available.

"But—a *big* but—the editor of the *Chicago Tribune* has been smitten by the charm of our friend Israel. He was ordered to be smitten by Gamaliel Hicks. Gamaliel owns the *Tribune* as well as the *Indianapolis Star*, the *Cincinnati Herald*, and some other very big Midwestern papers. Our hero hails from those parts. Gamaliel owns flour mills, all the railroads in northern Indiana, and several state legislatures. He supplements their salaries for favors which I can leave to your imagination. So, you see, some senators are beholden to him, as well as three or four governors."

"Go on," said Slocum.

"Horton keeps greyhounds. He has two Arabian mares. When he was twenty-five he was brevetted brigadier general, the youngest man to attain that rank in the American army. He drank deeply of glory and got to love the taste of it. When the war ended the cup was snatched from his lips. He reverted to his permanent rank of colonel. He did not like this at all, even though the good people of Indianapolis presented him with a saber in a rosewood case after the war.

"Well, all that ended. He has been a colonel for seventeen years now. The famous black curly locks are thinning. And where are there signs of war? Nowhere, friend Snow. Where are our enemies? We have none. And that means no promotions. And laurels—forgive me if I repeat myself— laurels are scarce along Indian trails.

"And now we can talk about his wife. I've seen her. A small, green-eyed woman, beautiful, sharp, and demanding.

French dresses and her own carriage. She brought quite a dowry with her, but all those mahogany banisters and a rack full of gold-headed canes—that takes money, money, money. If he should run for senator—and if he should get Hicks's support for that race—''

"Yes," Slocum said. "A nice way to top off a career."

"My friend," Cummings said, "senator is just a local stop. After two terms, why not run for number one? Washington was a colonel once, and look at Jackson, Tyler, Harrison, Grant! Even Lincoln was a lieutenant in the Black Hawk War."

"Yes,'' Slocum said, convinced.

"And do you know what that insolent whelp Palmer is doing every night? He's writing up the days adventures. When we get back he's sending it off to Hicks, and I've no doubt it'll be published in all his papers and a lot of Eastern papers will pick it up. Guess who will be the dashing hero in every single dispatch?"

"The Young Napoleon," Slocum said with a broad smile.

"Give the man a big seegar," Cummings said, suiting the action to the words. He handed a foul-smelling stogie to Slocum, who accepted it politely.

"Now," Cummings said, "we reach the end of this long speech of mine. And the point. No one has heard much of the Young Napoleon since the war. There was a small skirmish on a dawn raid on the Arickaree against the Cheyenne, and Hicks puffed up that one for all it was worth. But if he should ever run for office the Democrats will prove that the dead were mostly women and children, with a few old men thrown in while the warriors were out on a buffalo hunt.

"But Apaches!

"There we have something of vintage quality. Crook made 'em come in a couple of years ago, but Crook never had Horton's war record, now, did he? The Apaches are out again. It just so happens their lands will make fine grazing land, and there's plenty of silver to take out of their mountains—but they have to be pried out first. They torture in a horrible manner, praise the Lord! A large puffing can be made out of Apaches. Not like those poor harmless Diggers out in California. But if they should be spanked on their own reservation, surrounded by white ranchers, with railroads providing easy movement of troops and supplies, where's the glory? It would be like shooting fish in a barrel, and just about as dangerous. Not at all likely to make a man a senator.

"But listen closely. Suppose they should be forced off their reservation in large numbers. Suppose further that they should go to ground somewhere where a man would have to pry 'em out in a manner that would be dangerous and expensive in lives lost. What then? The medals would fall like rain, that's what! Newspapers all across Arizona would be dragging out their biggest typefaces for the occasion. Delegations full of gratitude will go to Washington. The *Chicago Tribune* and the other papers will not only reprint the Arizona papers, they'll run Palmer's special stories from the field with banner headlines.

"And the editorial pages will be full of thoughtful pieces about how a man with such organizational abilities should not be lost to the nation, that the halls of Congress—"

"Wait a minute," Slocum said. He sat upright, cross-legged, with easy grace. "One thing I want to know here."

"Shoot," said Cummings, with a casual wave of his hand. Slocum saw that the man was a little drunk and quite bitter; he managed to conceal this well under a surface of light banter.

"How do you know all this?" he asked.

"One," Cummings said, putting down his drink and ticking off the points on his fingers, "one, friend Snow, after many a year studying the man like a slug under a microscope, I know how his mind works. And, two, if that isn't good enough for you, the telegrapher told me.''

"You mean the telegrapher analyzed the situation and gave you his considered judgment?''

"Refrain from sarcasm, friend Snow,'' Cummings said. "The telegrapher told me—off the record, of course—that Horton had sent a long telegram to Headquarters, Department of Missouri, demanding that he be permitted to effect an immediate arrest of Nachodise, their medicine man, as the only possible way to prevent an uprising and to cool off the tribe in the tense situation prevailing. Those were the pearls of wisdom carved by our master's ruby-red lips.''

"Pearls are not carved.''

"Secreted then. Secreted by our master's secret lips.''

"But that would be the best way to set 'em off!'' Slocum said sharply.

"Precisely. By provoking the uprising, since he would be the senior officer on the spot, he would have to go out and suppress it. And then, with this swan song under his belt, he would retire.''

"And,'' Slocum said thoughtfully, "with the papers watching over him like a mother hen—''

"He's on his way to the White House,'' Cummings finished.

"He seems to have been very lucky all his life,'' Slocum said.

"Yep,'' Cummings said. The liquor had numbed his lips. "Yep. All his life. The roulette wheel can spin just once more for him, can't it? That's all he asks—can't that li'l ball go where he wants just once more?''

"That's not much to ask,'' Slocum said, smiling. Cummings was funny when he was drunk.

"Well, then,'' Cummings said heavily, "he'll need all the luck he can get. And so will we. So will we.''

Slocum knew what the man meant. It was rough enough

fighting Apaches in the Territory, where the surrounding population supported the troops. Fighting them in Mexico, without railroad or telegraphic support, with a hostile Mexican army circling around them with intentions that were not friendly either, was really loading the dice somewhat too heavily against Horton and his plans. It meant that every man in the command was in serious danger.

5

"How does he look?" asked Cummings.

Eskiminzin grunted. It was his usual way of indicating that he preferred not to give an opinion.

"Oh, come on!" Cummings said with an irritated air.

It was clear to Slocum that the two were old friends and could speak to each other with frankness.

"Well?" asked Cummings, holding his forehead flat against both palms. He had a splitting headache from the previous night's heavy drinking.

"No good," the Indian replied.

" 'No good, no good'," Cummings mimicked. "Don't be so goddamned inscrutable!"

"He's not able to walk as far as a fat pig, he's scareda snakes, he's 'fraida the men. No good."

"One of the bravest men I ever knew," Slocum said, "used to have the shakes so bad after a battle that he needed help to get up on his horse. After that he was fine."

Eskiminzin shook his head. He had other opinions. Cummings dropped the discussion and watched the village they were nearing. Its name was *Alamo Huaco*, or Crooked Cottonwood, from the ancient cottonwood that grew beside an old well whose windlass went down three hundred feet before it reached some alkaline but still drinkable water. They could have all they wanted, said its guardian, a little Mexican boy of eight. The price was a quarter for a horse or mule, ten cents per man. The little boy was in charge of a yoke of patiently chewing brown oxen.

Cummings beat him down to a nickel for the animals and nothing for the men. The captain enjoyed the bargaining as much as the boy.

After they had watered they moved on, amused by the flash of white curtains across the windows whenever they looked inside a house where a pretty girl might be looking out.

They began to move upward again, high into the ranges. Hundreds of thousands of pine trees grew so high above them that they looked like little black pins all jammed together. Slowly a pattern had worked itself out: Slocum and Cummings rode together, just behind the scout. Frequently Eskiminzin would drop back and confer briefly with Cummings, then move up again. Horton was a mile to the rear with the command, chatting with his nephew or with some other of the sycophants who were busily buttering him up by listening gratefully to his observations on the country, or to his experiences in the War. Rigby, the orderly, followed close on the colonel's heels, "like a goddamned fawning spaniel," as Cummings put it.

The wind rose and the dust smarted at their eyes. Everything had a hazy, filthy look, as if an enormous basin of dirty dishwater had been emptied over the countryside, which had then dried up. Up ahead, on the point's left flank, was a thick stand of pines.

Cummings ordered them to ride there for shelter from the coming thunderstorm, which could be violent at these altitudes. A few enormous, warm drops splattered against their faces. The horses were pricking their ears at the distant thunder.

Lightning flashed. Eskiminzin said, in Apache, "Ha! Thunder's friend!" The three men trotted quickly toward the pines. The Apache touched Cummings's arm and pointed to their rear.

Half a mile behind them he saw a cloud of dust through which rifle barrels and bridle bits were flashing. They must have come out of a narrow gully.

"Up to the pines!" Cummings ordered. They forced the horses hard. Hooves drummed in the mud as they spurred for shelter and a good defense position. They made it to the trees as the downpour reached its height.

"Dismount!"

They tied their horses forty feet to the rear of the grove. They crawled to the edge, cursing the steady drip from the pine needles onto their necks, and watched the Mexicans move up the trail, huddled in their serapes, with the patient air of people who were long used to suffering. For a moment Slocum hoped that the Mexicans might pass by their horses' tracks.

But one of them halted abruptly. He looked at the ground, rode briefly back and forth, and then pointed triumphantly up toward their hiding place.

"Son of a bitch," Cummings muttered. There was only one way out on horseback, and the Mexicans held that road. "Christ!"

Slocum dismounted. "What're you doing?" Cummings asked sharply.

"Make a barricade," Slocum said, beginning to drag broken and dead branches so that they formed barriers between the pines. "At least they can't ride us down."

Cummings grunted in approval. He placed a warning hand on Eskiminzin's arm as the Apache levered a cartridge into the chamber. "Maybe they only want to talk," he began, but there followed the crash of a rifle volley. Bark chips flew everywhere like startled grasshoppers.

"I'll bet you they've called on business," Slocum said with a smile. Action always exhilarated him. What made this particular encounter special was that he was in uniform for the first time since 1865.

"Don't shoot!" Cummings ordered the Apache, who glowered in resentment under his heavy brows.

"They shoot *us!*" Eskiminzin said.

"I'm not going to be the one who starts an international incident," Cummings said stiffly. Slocum smiled at Eskiminzin's puzzled face. He did not know what "international" meant—and frontiers meant nothing to nomadic tribes anyway.

"Suppose we have to shoot to get out of here?" Slocum asked reasonably.

"Let Horton straighten out this mess," Cummings said, flat on his belly on the damp earth. "He's heard the shooting. He's sure to be coming up fast. Let's just sit tight for a while."

Another ragged volley crashed. More bits of bark exploded, and one stung Cummings on the cheek. He swore automatically. Neither he nor Slocum knew that Horton had not heard the firing because of the heavy, mist-filled air and the several ridges that lay between the advance and the main body. Slocum lay with his face pressed flat. It was safe enough, with the wild firing, which was designed to force them to lift their heads.

"Snow, how's your old colonel up at Fort Grant?"

Slocum's face was impassive. This was the first time anyone had brought up the subject of his regiment.

"What do you mean, how is he?" Slocum said lightly. "He's better than some colonels and worse than others."

"I know *that,* for God's sake," Cummings said. "I mean, how fat is the fat old bastard? Gerard weighed two hundred and thirty pounds last time I saw him, about three months ago. He needed a Percheron at parade. Did he put on any more weight?"

Slocum took a chance and said, "Nope. Still at two-thirty."

Cummings rolled to one side and hoisted himself on an elbow. "It won't do, Snow," he said gently. "The Third never had a fat colonel, and certainly none named Gerard. So what's your game?"

Slocum had to trust Cummings. Something about the way he asked gave him confidence. So he told him the truth. He even told him that he had broken out of the Territorial Penitentiary.

Cummings laughed uproariously.

"How did you guess?" Slocum asked.

"I knew you'd been an officer," Cummings said, gasping for breath while he wiped a dirty handkerchief across his face. He had laughed so hard that he had cried. "But it was obvious that you hadn't been one for a long time. The look of surprise on your face when the colonel ordered a certain maneuver, as if you had forgotten it. The way you were a little awkward with the McClellan saddle the first few times you put it on. Things like that."

"What are you going to to about it?"

"Not a goddamn thing, friend Snow. When we get out of this stupid mess Horton put us into, I'm going to see that you leave us with a decent carbine and a good horse. I'll see to it that someone'll be on guard duty who'll not be averse to taking a little nip about two A.M. And I'll be the one offering him the nip. I wouldn't want your departure challenged by an anxious sentry who might pull down on you. I couldn't afford to lose a single enlisted man, not to mention a Johnny Reb I'd like to become my friend when I get out of this rotten little army. So we'll not mention the subject any more. Just let me know what night you'll be forsaking the hospitality of Colonel Horton's command."

"Well, I do appreciate it," Slocum said slowly.

"I suppose you can't tell me your real name."

"Nope," Slocum said agreeably.

"I thought not," Cummings said, grinning. "Maybe some day?"

"Maybe."

The Mexicans began firing more heavily. "Look sharp!" Cummings said. "They're up to something!"

"You don't think they'll charge?" Slocum asked.

"No. Suicidal up this steep slope. So *that's* it!"

They were trying to set fire to the pines. If it hadn't been for the rain the trees would have flared up like skyrockets. Soon they gave up. One of them called out, "Hello! Come, we friends, we talk!"

"Sure," Cummings muttered. He drew his forefinger across his throat.

It began to grow dark as the sun sank behind the western ridge. Slocum knew that if they stayed there during the night their lines would be infiltrated on all sides. It was simple tactics, and their commander did not look like a fool, even though he insisted on dragging that woman around with him.

"What's your plan?" Slocum asked.

"Outsit them," Cummings said. "They'll get tired soon enough and go off to new pastures."

"I beg to differ," Slocum said politely.

Cummings waved a hand, granting permission to differ. Slocum thought of all the officers he had met with superior rank who would have barked an order to shut up. He liked Cummings even more.

"I know this country and I know Mexicans," Slocum said. "They have their honor at stake. They're not going to go away. They're staying. They won't leave till we're dead or until we surrender. The ground is getting wetter; soon when they come we won't even hear them coming."

"Well?" Cummings asked.

"We retreat."

"Horton wouldn't like that at all."

"Horton's ass is not on the line here. To stay is stupid. We can always fight another day," Slocum reasoned.

"There's no way we can take the horses up over the mountain. No way."

"We abandon the horses."

Cummings stared, openmouthed. It was unheard of to abandon cavalry mounts. If a man were afoot just about anywhere in the West, he died soon after. No one could walk such great distances, no one could outrun a mounted enemy or face an enraged bull afoot.

"But Snow—"

"Don't you see? There's no way we can survive a night attack. They're sure we won't abandon the horses. So they won't have placed sentries in back of us. They can have the horses, and we'll just disappear and live to fight another day."

"But, technically—"

"It's desertion. Yes, I know." He grinned.

"Snow, it's not a problem for you," Cummings began. Then he too grinned. "Oh, why the hell not?" he said. "I'll never get my goddamn promotion anyway. I might as well have some fun watching him get all purple. Sure. Let's go. Take all your ammunition. A shame to lose those nice saddles. We'll fire a couple volleys to make 'em keep their heads down, and as soon as we're done with that little housekeeping chore we'll go up the hill. All set? *Fire!*"

The volleys crashed under the rain-drenched pines. A few crows who had thought the shooting was over for the night flew upward in spirals, cawing furiously. Then the three men climbed up the mountain. The pine needles made the hillside as slippery as glass.

"Quiet!" muttered Cummings. "They'll hear us! Quiet!"

Their hands became sticky from the fragrant pine sap as they clutched at branches to pull themselves up in the darkness. They crawled over fallen trees and forced their way through the incredible tangles of branches that resulted when one tree had fallen across another one. Panting, they waded through ice-cold streams, and as they paused to catch their breath there came five ringing volleys in succession.

"The final charge," Slocum said.

There were no more shots. "A good thing I listened to you, Snow. They would have wiped us out," Cummings said.

They pushed on for two more hours. It was too hard to move in the dark, without stars to show direction. Cummings halted on the top of a hill for the night. They shivered through the damp air to a dim, pearly-white dawn. They could see wisps of chill mist and fog drifting through the tops of the pines. They picked their way down to an arroyo and followed its tortuous, winding course. It debouched into a small canyon, and no sooner had they entered it when a voice shouted from above, *"Manos arriba!* Hands up!" Rifle barrels appeared suddenly on the canyon rim. Escape was impossible.

"Shit!" Cummings said feelingly. "The bastards figured we'd come out here, and just rode around to wait for us."

"Rifles on the ground!" came the next order.

"Put 'em down," Cummings said wearily. From behind a boulder strode Don Gabriel, with a wide grin on his face.

Their hands were tied behind their backs. Three men brought up their own horses, and the prisoners were helped on.

"Very neat," Slocum said with admiration. "A nice touch."

Cummings stared at him, then broke out laughing. "I've been in worse messes, Snow," he observed, "but never with someone with as casual an approach as you. It's very relaxing."

"When I relax, so do my guards," Slocum said. "And it's easier to get by a relaxed guard than one whose back is up because his prisoner hates him and is obviously plotting something.''

"Damned if you're not right, Snow," Cummings said admiringly.

Eskiminzin was quiet. Slocum turned to look. The Apache's eyes glittered like shiny black agates as he stared at the Mexicans. His guard returned the hatred with interest.

Slocum said, "But there's no way any Apache is going to look relaxed in front of a Mexican."

"I'm afraid you're right," Cummings agreed.

Beside Don Gabriel rode a very clever guide, a man named Ibarruri, a Mexican of Basque descent. Ibarruri's jaw looked as if it had been broken in three places and badly fitted together after. Someone had hit it with a sledgehammer in a miner's dispute. He was a convicted murderer, Don Gabriel explained politely to Cummings, who had been temporarily released because he was as skillful as any Yaqui or Apache in tracking. Indeed, Don Gabriel went on, it had been Ibarruri's idea that the retreat of the two Americans and the Apache would be up to the crest of the mountain and thence down to the arroyo. So they had ridden all night and set up the ambush just where Ibarruri had indicated.

"He did very well, no?" Don Gabriel asked. "If he continues to do well, he will be pardoned. He loves his wife; if he tries to escape she will go to prison. She is very pretty and the jailers are hard to control—you see?" He smirked with self-satisfaction as he made his logic clear. "So Ibarruri—" the man jerked his head as he heard his name mentioned—"is a *very* good tracker. He knew you would circle around and head for the command."

Don Gabriel was bored, he told Cummings. He would much prefer to be in Mexico City than in the accursed north. In Mexico City there were French girls and champagne. Here in the north there was nothing but scorpions and pulque. The distances were too great, the mountains too high, the rebels too serious. And the Apaches—the Apaches were evil and vengeful.

It was not often that they managed to catch one. He and Ibarruri looked with tightened, hard mouths at Eskiminzin, who returned their look. Slocum did not give much chance for Eskiminzin to get out of this alive. Eskiminzin was aware of this too, and his hard black stare was full of the acid hatred of three hundred years of war to the knife.

Don Gabriel was fighting the perpetual Mexican war: federal troops against rebels. In this war, incidents such as the French attempt in the 1860s to set up an empire under Maximilian, or the American seizure of Vera Cruz and Mexico City, were simply small, brief interludes in which everyone was allowed to shoot at the invaders and no harm done. Or all parties could use the presence of the invaders as propaganda in internal politics. It was always understood, added Don Gabriel, who was unusually expansive because of his triumph in taking prisoners by his strategy, that as soon as the foreigners left the country, the Mexicans could then get down to the really serious business of shooting each other.

"Therefore," Don Gabriel concluded, with a wide movement of his outstretched arms, "you see you are really unimportant, you Americans. Yes. The grand game is being played against General Duarte, who controls quite a bit of Chihuahua indeed. Mostly mountains. Wild Yaquis, too. They give him much trouble."

He grinned.

He seemed to Slocum to be a rather intelligent fellow. Maybe he deserved that handsome woman who had been riding around after his little army. Slocum wondered idly if he would get to see her before Don Gabriel did what he was planning to do, which could very well involve being stood up against a wall.

Maybe Cummings had an idea that would be coming up, maybe not. If Slocum became sure that would be the end for them, he would make his move with Cummings and Eskiminzin. There would be no point right now in alerting Cummings. The man might make a desperate move before the time was ripe. Time enough later.

They were moving now into more populated country. A few isolated ranches became visible in the valleys, which were broad and gently sloping. It was well watered country, too. They saw deer everywhere. No wonder the Apaches resisted the Spanish invasion so long ago, with its inevitable result that they were pushed backward and upward into the harsh mountain climate.

Ibarruri always rode in advance. His eyes wandered from the trail to the backs of distant moving cattle, then back again to the trail at his feet.

Once he said, "Five horses have passed ahead of us about an hour ago. Two are led, one had two men on its back." Slocum knew he was right when they caught up with the group he had described. Once he saw a man on a hillside trail ahead and to the right of the trail. He pulled out his carbine and disappeared at a gallop into the chaparral. They met him again an hour later, waiting for them on the trail, with his prisoner's rifle under his arm, and beaming upon the stunned man, who knew he would be shot later that day.

The trial lasted less than a minute. The rebel was pulled from his horse, slapped on the back, and told to run. He made a frantic run for the chaparral and Ibarruri carefully squeezed his trigger. Then he pumped out the empty cartridge with a wide grin while he murmured, *"Bueno, bueno!"*

The message was not lost upon Cummings, who paled. Cummings had never been a prisoner or a captive during his entire army career, and he was plunged into despair, although he concealed it well. Slocum, for whom such setbacks were almost routine, wasted no time worrying.

His eyes roamed everywhere, seeking a way out or a careless handler of a gun—anything which could be seized for an advantage. But nothing was apparent . . . so far.

6

Late that afternoon they reached Tecolote. The prisoners were kicked into a one-room adobe cell. The town had no jail, and the unfortunate *mestizo* and his family who lived there had been summarily thrown out. They sat on the edge of the village, quietly passive, but the arrogance of the act had simply recruited another eventual rebel. The villagers collected and threw stones into the hut, but it was Eskiminzin they were trying to hit. The hut had a door on its east side so that it would face the rising sun. A sentry was placed in front—Ibarruri. The man's motivation was enough for the position. He knew quite well what would happen to him and to his wife if the prisoners should escape.

The three prisoners sat on the dirt floor. Don Gabriel rode up. Slocum could see him, framed in the opening. He gave a curt command; Ibarruri pulled Slocum to his feet and gave him a brutal shove so that he stumbled. His hands were lashed tightly at his wrists with a piece of rawhide. As Slocum fell he twisted his head sideways so that he took the force of the fall on his left cheek. The soil was packed hard by the vicious sun and his cheekbone was scraped raw. As he struggled to his knees, Slocum turned to look at Ibarruri. His face was as impassive as Eskiminzin's. Slocum knew how to wait.

When he looked at Don Gabriel his attention immediately shifted to the woman. She sat her horse with the casual, natural ease of someone whose ancestors had been *vaqueros* for centuries. She sat astride her mare, a practice frowned upon in polite circles in the capital. But then, Slocum could see that she was not a woman who would fit into the artificial conventions of such a society, but that she also would not give a damn. She stared at him with much more than polite interest. It would have been described as a bold look, if she had been moving in an elegant party at the capital, but this woman did not play games. Her interest in him was clearly, frankly sexual.

She saw a man over six feet tall, pared of all fat to the bone, with a hard face and compressed lips. His bright green eyes made a vivid contrast to his deeply tanned face. As he looked at her, his lips relaxed into a pleased smile. She liked that. He wore a uniform which had once been blue, but was now faded and torn. The yellow stripes along the legs identified him as a cavalry officer. The only other Americans she had ever seen had been brawling cowpunchers or engineers from occasional locomotive trains with wads of chewing tobacco bulging their cheeks. They had leered at her and made suggestive remarks. This one returned her stare with a look of frank admiration, and she liked that.

She also liked the fact that he showed no fear whatsoever. She closed her right hand into a fist and rested her knuckles on her right hip. This gesture thrust her breasts forward, as she knew very well it would. Slocum's eyes dropped to her breasts and lingered slowly over their fullness. She felt her pulse beat more strongly. She liked this little smile. It promised competence in lovemaking—something her protector, Don Gabriel, was deficient in. He liked to display her as his Indian trophy, in order to excite envy in his colleagues, who were forced to content themselves on the march with a quick lay in some squalid brothel.

In private, however, he was capable of no subtlety or staying power in the sexual act. Their encounters naturally left her restless, unsatisfied, sullen, and ready to look with favor upon anyone who looked as if he might have more staying power.

But the problem was that Don Gabriel was fanatically jealous and possessive. He was completely capable of killing anyone he found in her bed. This would not be much of a problem if they were stationed at any army post near some town, where she could meet men who were not in the army, and who would be willing to risk death on the slight chance that they might be discovered with her.

But on the march the only people with whom she came in contact were soldiers under Don Gabriel's command. No matter how passionately they might desire her, they certainly would not risk death for that; and if they were officers, even if they escaped death, their careers would come to an abrupt halt. Any soldier seeing a civilian who was considering a leap into her bed would quickly put a halt to it out of simple envy.

But here was someone who didn't fit into either category—a soldier from another army, and one who had nothing to lose.

Don Gabriel had not noticed any of this almost imperceptible byplay. "You are here without permission, *señor*," he said. "It is quite possible that you have been contemplating giving rifles to the rebels. I feel that evidence proving this traitorous act is easily acquired. This is an offense punishable by the firing squad in Mexico. Would you like to remark upon this, *señor?*"

"I am not the senior officer," Slocum said. He indicated Cummings with a jerk of his head.

"That may be," Don Gabriel said idly, "but you speak excellent Spanish, *señor*. I prefer to talk to you."

"Captain."

"*Señor?*" Don Gabriel asked politely.

"Captain. My rank. I am a captain in the army of the United States. I would prefer that you use the title."

"Idiot! What you prefer and what I shall call you are very clearly two separate things, *señor*."

Now that Don Gabriel's gaze was rigidly fixed upon Slocum's face, the woman rubbed her left thumb across her left nipple. Slocum watched it harden and bulge against the thin cotton fabric. In spite of the dangerous situation he felt anticipation and excitement. She lifted her eyebrows in a questioning look. The message was clear.

Slocum nodded slowly. Satisfied that her query had been answered in the affirmative, she smiled and then stretched her arms wide and yawned. Her red tongue came out and she licked at her full, red lips.

Don Gabriel said, irritated, "If you are bored, my dear, please go away. I have business with this man, and then I shall get rid of him."

"Get rid of?" she asked.

"Tomorrow, with the others. I shall show them what invading Mexico means. Now go to sleep if you are bored!"

She shrugged, turned her horse, and rode off.

"Women!" Don Gabriel said with a comradely smile, just as if he and Slocum shared a secret. "Now I am going to get some sleep, *señor*. Tomorrow you and that other *señor* will have something to think about. *Buenas noches.*"

Ibarruri pulled Slocum to his feet with effortless ease, spun him around, and kicked him. Slocum stumbled back into the adobe hut and crashed against its back wall. The dried mud, six inches thick and mixed with straw, was hard as a rock to the front of his skull. Slocum shook his head, dazed, and slowly sank to his knees.

"Unpleasant fellow," Cummings said. "What the hell did that pompous ass want?"

"He wants us to admit that we came down here to stir up a rebellion."

"Fool."

"Also he won't call us captains."

"Petty bastard. How's your head?"

"Banged somewhat. I'd like to be alone with that miserable bastard who's been shoving me in and out of this hut."

Eskiminzin said nothing. He peered outside, where two soldiers had begun digging a hole. At first Slocum thought they were digging a grave, but Eskiminzin knew better. The hole was only two feet square and went straight down for six feet. He began a low chanting as the hole got deeper.

"Oh, shut up!" Cummings said nervously to the Indian.

"It's his death song," Slocum said quietly. He knew what the hole was for. It was an old Apache custom that the Mexicans had adopted. In the hut it was windless and hot, even though the sun had set. The soldiers kept digging. When it was dark, someone brought a lantern and they dug by its light. Eskiminzin kept up his droning chant. He sang all night long.

In the morning they came for him. None of the three had slept. By seven A.M. the temperature must have reached eighty-five. In an hour it would be ninety, and by noon it would be one hundred twenty in the open, where the hole had been dug. Sand flies, beetles, horseflies, gnats, mosquitoes, and scorpions had already begun their tiny, deadly combats.

A shabby lieutenant headed the squad. He had a sword which kept getting between his legs. Slocum had experienced things like this before, where farce was intermingled with tragedy. Ibarruri trailed the squad, munching with gusto on a chicken leg as he watched the squad drag the Apache out of the hut. They dragged Eskiminzin across the hard-packed earth to the hole and slid him in. When he was standing up inside, the ground was at his neck level. Ibarruri said, yelling towards the hut, "Pretty good, no? I measured good!"

The soil was filled in. Ibarruri stamped down hard with his feet till the dirt was packed solidly around the Apache.

The lieutenant helped enthusiastically. His spurs scraped Eskiminzin's face with brutal unconcern. Slocum felt rage flood over him. He had liked Eskiminzin's quiet competence on the march. Cummings had not had much experience on the frontier, and the Mexicans' casual savagery rattled him. He turned his head to one side in his helplessness. He did not want to look.

Slocum was made of harder material. He watched everything with an almost clinical detachment. He wanted to remember it all. Slocum did not forgive injuries that were deliberately done. He filed everything away in his brain. Payment was slow but sure in Slocum's personal scheme of things.

So he watched while Ibarruri poured a jar of honey over Eskiminzin's head. In fifteen minutes the Apache's head was a black mass of flies, gnats, and beetles. Scorpions came out from under rocks and moved like gray ghosts among the smaller insects. Eskiminzin made no sound. He had sung his death song; he had calmly accepted that he would die in agony. But one thing Slocum was sure of—Eskiminzin would make no sound. His enemy would get no pleasure from that. He would die in honorable silence.

Cummings's jaw muscles kept pulsing. Slocum suddenly realized that the captain was praying. It was not what he expected. But Cummings was not repeating "The Lord is my shepherd." He was praying for vengeance. Slocum liked him for that.

At two that afternoon a guard brought the two American officers a pitcher of water and two tortillas apiece. With the inconsistent behavior which frequently puzzled Slocum when dealing with Mexicans, the guard held the tortillas to their lips while they chewed and swallowed. Then he held the pitcher for them while they drank their fill. Slocum suddenly realized what it all meant. People who were about to be executed were treated gently.

By dusk the Indian's head barely moved. Eskiminzin's tongue protruded. It was so swollen that it had poked itself between his teeth. He could not close his mouth. The tongue was covered with mosquitoes.

Suddenly Slocum became aware of a faint scratching sound behind him, as if a mouse were gnawing at the adobe. The noise went on, too faint to be heard by the sentry outside.

Ten minutes later he felt a thin draft at his wrists where they were bound together. Someone had made a hole. A hand slid in and tugged at his sleeve. He bent down and pressed his ear against it.

The woman said softly, "I will distract the sentry. When you go out, go to the right to the edge of the village. North along the river you will see, a hundred yards maybe, a big old willow tree. Wait for me there. Do you promise?"

"Yes," he whispered.

"Not good enough," she said softly. "Word of honor? What you do afterwards is your business. But this you will do as you promise. Yes or no?"

"Word of honor," Slocum said softly. A knife slid into the opening and cut his bonds. He put his hands in his lap and massaged them. Several seconds later he heard a faint cry and then a thud. By then Slocum was at the door, moving so quietly that the uneasily sleeping Cummings did not hear him.

She had pretended to fall. The sentry stared in her direction. "*Oye!*" she called out. "I fell and twisted my ankle, *amigo*. Help me to my bed."

"*Señorita*, I cannot leave my post. I—"

"Help me, or I shall inform Don Gabriel that you let me lie here in pain," she insisted.

The man was torn by indecision. She let out a muffled cry of pain. That convinced the sentry. He walked to her, helped her up, and, with her arm around his shoulders, they moved slowly and carefully to her hut.

Slocum drifted out of the opening as silently as smoke. Using the shadows for cover, he moved around the houses and edged around the small plaza. A dog started to bark at him. He threw a stone at it and then silenced it with a well-directed blow to its ribs, and so moved to the edge of the village. The little stream ran quietly past the village. Slocum clung to its banks as he moved north to the huge willow. When he arrived he looked upward. The trunk was nearly twenty feet in circumference. Slocum knew that it must be at least as old as the village—four hundred years seemed a fair estimate of its age. Its trunk was heavily convoluted, with massive branches like buttresses angling out from the trunk. There was room between any two of them for a bed to be placed, Slocum thought, as he sat down and waited for her.

The night was chilly, a stunning contrast to the broiling heat of the day. Eskiminzin was still buried up to his neck. That was unfinished business to be taken care of as soon as he had fulfilled his obligation to the woman.

He heard a soft whistle and froze. Maybe it was the woman, maybe it wasn't. He was not going to make the first move.

"Captain?" she whispered.

When he moved out she gasped, startled. She was holding a thick woolen *reboza* in her arms. "You move like a big cat," she whispered. In truth, all of his moves were like oiled pistons sliding inside cylinders: easy, effortless, sinuous.

"Come!" she whispered again. She had sunk to the ground and spread out her *reboza*. He unbuttoned his tunic. She knelt and put her face against his groin. His penis swelled at the contact. She laid her cheek against it and said, "You please me. Not like my friend. He moves like a wild pig. In bed, a goat. Fast, fast. Then he snores. But you are a *tigre!*

"I will be very quiet," she whispered. *"Very* quiet. Usually I make much noise, as if a man were beating me, but that is only my way of showing pleasure. The louder I scream the bigger my pleasure. It is simple, is it not? But here to scream would be stupid. You would be killed."

There was no question about that, Slocum knew. He was about to screw a very passionate lady, but it had to be done in silence. A few hundred yards back in the village Eskiminzin was buried up to his neck and Cummings was snoring restlessly.

But if that was the price to pay to get all three of them out of this mess, it was perfectly all right with him.

As for getting past the sentry and digging out Eskiminzin, all in good time. First things first.

"You would be killed," she repeated as she unbuttoned his pants. She looked up at his hard face.

"Maybe not," she added. "Maybe you would kill them first. But of a certainty they would kill me—maybe not with you here, but of a certainty, later. But first Don Gabriel would give me to the men for a while, it would not be pleasant. So, then," she finished, with her white teeth flashing brilliantly in her tawny face, "I will be quiet. You will see. Very quiet."

She pulled her dress over her head. Underneath she was naked. She cupped her melon-shaped breasts in her palms and lifted them slightly. "I am very clean," she said. "I bathed an hour ago in the river." She teased his penis out from his pants and pressed her face against it. Slocum felt the heat radiating from her face as if it were a small oven. His penis swelled. She crooned with pleasure as she rubbed her cheek against it. She put a palm on his thigh. Even through the fabric of his trousers he could feel the heat of her hand.

"Oh, very good, very good," she murmured as she

brought up both palms and and stroked his penis between her palms. "Take off your clothes," she whispered.

Slocum stripped. He lay down beside her on the *reboza*. She reached across and pulled the top fold across them. The soft wool was very warm. She bent over him and let her nipples brush across his face. He took one nipple in his mouth and sucked it. She let out a long, shuddering sigh. Her right palm cupped his testicles and, stroking them with the tips of the fingers of her left hand, she gently touched his penis. She bent down and let her tongue dart in light, flicking touches along the shaft. Slocum writhed his hips in pleasure. She ran the hot end of her tongue up the length of his penis and down the other side. Then she pursed her mouth, licked her lips till they were moist, and very slowly slid her mouth down his shaft till her throat could take no more of its length. Then she slowly withdrew. Then she went down again, each time gradually increasing the speed. Finally Slocum could hold back no longer. He burst in a long, powerful orgasm and she swallowed the hot jet of liquid, moaning and wriggling her moistened thighs as she sucked up every drop.

Exhausted, Slocum lay back on the *reboza*. She smiled down at him. Even though he had just escaped from the hut, he would have liked nothing more than to sleep.

But she was not yet satisfied. Gently she stroked his limp penis, again and again, till it began to grow stiff. Up and down she began licking and sucking at it till it was as big as it had been. Then she straddled him and began to ride him, but in a subtle variation he had never come across before.

She slid down on the purple, engorged head only for half an inch. Then she went up till her vagina just cleared it, then down again for half an inch. Then up again, then down again. The effect was that of great, tantalizing tension, delightful, and it increased the feeling of pleasant anticipation enormously for both of them. Suddenly, without warning, she plunged down as hard as she could, then up again, where she teased him with her technique. Then she plunged downward till she hit his groin with an audible slap. "This is called 'the tailor's needle,' " she said in his ear, bending down as she wriggled around and around, her juices flowing down along his penis. "Do you like it?" Her breasts swayed heavily above him in the darkness. She held her right breast in one hand and thrust the nipple in his mouth while she rode him like a rider on a stallion. Slocum had never tried that particular variation before, and he could not hold himself in. Once more he exploded. She started to scream, but he clapped a palm over her mouth. She bit his forefinger as hard as she could while her hips writhed in a violent frenzy of thrashing.

Then she slumped, exhausted, against his chest.

There was another sentry on duty when Slocum drifted back. He stood in the shadow of one of the huts while he debated with himself on his next step. She had refused to distract the man on watch again. "Once is a big risk," she said lazily as she rested her head against Slocum's thigh. "Twice is too dangerous. No. You will have to do it yourself. Good luck. Maybe we shall meet again. Till then, *adios*." She stood up and pulled her dress over her head, picked up the *reboza*, brushed the dust off, and wrapped it around her head and shoulders. She looked like any other Indian woman. Then she cupped his balls tenderly, sighed and smiled, and moved silently away in the darkness.

Slocum watched her go. He had no complaints. She would have trouble enough explaining to Don Gabriel why she had asked the sentry to help her. It would be clear that this had given the American the opportunity to flee. Slocum wished her luck.

The new sentry seemed much more vigilant than the other. He looked around frequently as he walked back and forth. There would be no stealing up on him. He would give

the alarm too readily. A tinkle sounded under Slocum's
right toe. He looked down. It was an empty *pulque* bottle.
It gave him an idea. He picked it up and filled it half full
of water from the creek. Then he began moving with an
alcoholic stagger toward the sentry. From time to time he
upended the bottle and pretended to take a long swallow.
He sang a Mexican drinking song:

> *"Do you know pulque?*
> *A divine liquor!*
> *Angels drink it*
> *In the evening!"*

The guard laughed quietly. From the dim light that came
from the rising moon Slocum could see that the new sentry
was Ibarruri. *"Una bebida, amigo?"* Slocum called out as
he waved toward Ibarruri.

"Como no?" In the dim light Slocum could see the dark
round ball that was Eskiminzin's head. Something wet
stained one cheek. Slocum thought it was blood. Something seemed glued on the same cheek. Slocum couldn't
quite make it out, since Ibarruri was extending an arm for
the *pulque*.

"Take it!" Slocum said, and smashed the bottle against
Ibarruri's head. The man staggered for a moment, then
recovered. Blood streamed down his head. He grunted and
lurched blindly at Slocum. It was important to ensure that
he made no sound to alert anyone. Slocum lowered his
head and butted the man in the jaw as hard as he could. He
heard the jawbone crack. Ibarruri moaned and reached for
his sheath knife. It came out in a quick, fluid, practiced
move, with the point aimed upward in the traditional knife
fighter's stance. They circled in silence. For a second
Slocum wondered why Ibarruri had not called out for
assistance. Then he realized it must be because the man

prided himself on his ability to take care of any attacker without help.

Ibarruri's jaw, previously broken in an old scrap, was offset now; it had shifted half an inch to the left. It would heal in a grotesque fashion, given the haphazard technique of rural Mexican medicine. For a second Slocum almost felt sorry for the man. But when Ibarruri started to weave the knife in circles and feints, trying to distract Slocum away from what would be the final lunge, he forgot his compassion.

Coolly he moved backward, just out of range. They moved like partners in some exotic dance, linked together by the weaving sliver of silver that darted up like a rattlesnake's lunge, then fluttered down again like a falling leaf. Without being aware of what he was doing, Ibarruri had now moved close to Eskiminzin, who was still buried up to his neck. Slocum feinted at Ibarruri's face with the jagged neck of the bottle. Ibarruri stepped back six inches and Eskiminzin bit him in the ankle as hard as he could.

Startled, Ibarruri half turned. Unable to escape, he fell. Slocum was on him like a cougar. He kicked him in the side of his head with a thump that made Cummings, who was watching from inside the hut, wince. That did it. Ibarruri was unconscious. The fight had been finished in total silence.

Slocum picked up the knife, cut off Ibarruri's belt, and tied the man up. Dragging the sentry swiftly into the adobe hut, Slocum cut Cummings's bonds. Using the rawhide thongs, he quickly tore off a piece of Ibarruri's shirt, shoved it into his mouth, and tied it into place. The rest of the rawhide was used to tie his ankles together.

Outside, only a mongrel cur was interested in what they were doing as he and Cummings dug out Eskiminzin with their hands.

"Know what that bastard did?" Cummings whispered

as he pawed at the hard-packed dirt. "He kicked Eskiminzin in the eye as hard as he could. See?"

With a startled look, Slocum pivoted and stared at the Apache's face. His left eye hung out from the socket. As soon as his arms were freed, Eskiminzin helped them. When his knees were free, the big Apache strained and grunted and finally pulled himself up. He took his eye in his fingers and pushed the eye back in its socket. Slocum shuddered. Then the Apache walked toward the hut where Ibarruri lay.

"Jesus Christ!" breathed Cummings. "It's time we took off. For Christ's sake, stop him!"

"Not me," Slocum said.

"For God's sake, Snow!"

"They don't fight by our rules," Slocum said calmly. "I'm giving him three minutes alone with him. Then we're leaving."

"I've done my best to prevent acts of torture when I use Apache scouts—" Cummings began.

They heard a gasp and a moan inside the hut, then the sound of Ibarruri's body as it writhed and moved across the dirt floor in agony. Then came a long, stifled moan, then silence.

"Quick enough," Slocum whispered. Eskiminzin's right hand was wet with Ibarruri's blood. The Mexican would never have to worry any more about his wife being raped—or about anything else.

As they moved quietly along the village streets, Eskiminzin stolidly held his eye in place.

The moon had set. The sentry by the corral was so sure that he was in perfect safety that it was easy to disarm and gag him and tie him up securely.

They rode into the camp in a thin drizzle. A tall sentry in a slicker clicked his carbine and shouted, "Halt and dismount!"

They did. He came closer, and another sentry appeared at their rear and covered them with his carbine. Someone called out, "Where the devil have you fellows been?" Then, seeing the officers' shoulder straps, he disappeared in double-quick time. Another man cried out, "You all right, Captain?" and "Hey, you red devil!"

Cummings said, "Take care of these horses, will you?"

"Sure, Cap'n," grinned one of the slicker-clad men. "You want some hot coffee? It's all ready."

"Thanks, Corporal."

"These're stolen hosses, ain't they?" the corporal asked with a smile.

"A fair exchange is no robbery," Cummings replied.

"No exchange, Cap'n. We got yours right here. What you want me to do with this flea-bait?"

Cummings thought for a second. The Mexican horses were too small for the generally heavier American cavalrymen. The corporal held the reins and waited.

"You got ours all right?" Cummings asked.

"Yeah, we found 'em." He came closer. "The colonel," he said, dropping his voice, "went crazy when he couldn't find you up that arroyo. He chewed up the ground for six miles around, he was so mad. Yeah, your horse is all right." he added in a stilted, self-conscious tone. He had seen Colonel Horton striding furiously toward them.

"Let 'em go," Cummings said, jerking his head toward the three Mexican horses. There was nothing they could do with them. Some poor peon might find them and be happy to have them.

"What?" demanded Horton. "Did I hear you say to let those horses go? Are you crazy, Cummings?"

The sentries shuffled their feet in embarrassment. Quarrels between officers, although food for much fascinated discussion afterwards, shook the men's confidence in the figures whom they would have to follow on the battlefield.

"You ride away from the command, abandon your horses

and equipment. You come back a day later without so much as reporting to me, even with a fabricated story. You saw that we were riding into an ambush, and you ran away to save your skins without warning us. We lost four dead because of your cowardice. And now you want to return these horses to the enemy. Are you *mad?*"

His face red, Cummings said, "Sir, I—"

"Enough!" Horton shouted. "Corporal!"

"Sir!"

"Lead these horses up to that camp fire! On the double!"

Slocum followed Horton and the horses, feeling sorry for Cummings's public humiliation. Eskiminzin trailed along. His English was not good enough to follow every word, but he had heard enough to know that the captain had been shamed. During the night he had cut away his dangling eyeball. A glaring red socket stared out of his impassive, bronzed face. He had accepted this as calmly as a wolf would accept a broken leg in a trap.

In the embers of the camp fire three sentries had set up a coffee pot where the coffee was brewing, now forgotten.

"Put those goddamn horses on that side," Horton said.

"Yes, sir."

Horton withdrew his revolver. Walking to each horse in turn, he put bullets through their brains. He took, Slocum noticed, a particularly obscene pleasure in doing it. He shot each horse through its right eye.

"Good," the colonel said with satisfaction. "No use to *anyone* in this godforsaken country." The killings seemed to have relaxed him, Slocum saw. He holstered his gun.

"Now," he said almost pleasantly, as if a completely different man had been shouting at Cummings only minutes ago, "what information do you have on that greaser?"

He listened with a distinct lack of interest, as if he were forced to undergo a necessary and boring duty, while Cummings stiffly recited his estimate of the number of men under Don Gabriel's command, the condition of their rifles, how much ammunition they had, and whether the officers seemed competent or not.

When Cummings had finished, Horton remarked, "You look all right. Like you took a little vacation."

Cummings let that pass. "Sir," he said, "my scout lost an eye. I think he should be treated right away. There—"

"Never mind," Horton interrupted indifferently. "If he's lost it, he's lost it."

Slocum became aware that the man's speech was slightly slurred. He realized that Colonel Horton was a little drunk.

"Sir—for the record. So he can claim a pension."

"The hell with him. He's not any more use. Tell him to go home. Give him a sack of oats for the horse, and that's it."

"Sir," Cummings said, trying hard to keep the anger out of his voice, "he was promised his carbine for his services."

"Where's the carbine?"

"The Mexicans took it when we were jumped."

"You must be out of your mind, Cummings. He *lost* the goddamn gun. It was U.S. property. By rights I ought to make him pay for it. But who cares about the Mexicans? Important thing is the Apaches. I want to run down the red bastards. Run 'em into the ground! See to your troops; we're riding hard tomorrow. And as for you, Snow," he added, turning toward Slocum, "you'd better turn in. You'll take over Cummings's patrol if anything happens to him."

"Yes, sir," Slocum said politely. There was no reason to alienate the man, even though he resented his vicious, nagging treatment of Cummings. Time enough for dealing with Horton later.

Lieutenant Palmer emerged from the colonel's Sibley tent. Through the tent flap, as it was drawn back, Slocum could see three empty bottles of champagne. Horton went into his tent while Cummings, his jaw muscles still knotted from the tension of trying to keep his temper under control, stared at the half full bottle of champagne that was weighing down the open map on the table.

"The gentry live well even in the field," he said bitterly to Slocum. Slocum could well imagine what Mrs. Cummings used for carpets with his captain's pay—gunny sacks. He had heard that Mrs. Horton had brought along several Persian rugs with which she adorned the best house on Officers' Row. But then, she came from a wealthy family herself.

Palmer said thickly, "Cummings. Wanna talk t' you."

Cummings looked at him with distaste. "Talk," he grunted as he turned around.

Palmer stepped closer. "Must 'pologize poor habit not saluting," he said. He tittered. Then he raised his voice so that everyone for thirty feet around could hear him. "Fell off horse. Company A walked over small of back. Can't lift arm to salute."

In spite of his annoyance, Cummings smiled at the image.

"Whatcha grinnin' for? 'Struth." Palmer's voice had passed the bounds of drunken amiability and was now vicious.

Slocum watched him warily. He knew how drunks worked themselves up to perform unpleasant acts. One was being readied now. Cummings did not have this subtle awareness, and he was continuing to walk away.

"Good night, Lieutenant," Cummings said politely, but Palmer grabbed his elbow and spun him around. The men around the fire had stopped talking and were watching in silence.

"Know why I don't salute?" Palmer demanded.

"I don't know and I don't care," Cummings said sharply. "You're drunk. Get to your tent before you get into trouble."

" 'Cause you're not *worth* a salute. Thash why. Never

promoted, always jealous of better men than you, always backbiting—''

Cummings flushed. He tried to pull out of Palmer's grip, but the younger man was too strong.

''Lieutenant, if you please,'' Cummings said, almost in a whisper. His hand shaped itself around an imaginary gun butt. Slocum knew that, if pushed, the older man would pull his gun—and he might use it.

Slocum had nothing to lose. He stepped forward and slapped Palmer so hard that the man's head snapped to the left. One of the men sitting at the fire moaned in sympathy.

The silence that followed was so complete that Slocum could hear the fire crackling.

7

Colonel Horton said, "Snow, we'll take up this matter of your unprovoked attack on a brother officer later. I hope that's clear."

"Yes, sir," Slocum said. It was early the next morning.

Horton continued. "Captain Cummings is not in a very good condition to lead any scouts. You seem to know how to do that reasonably well." He lifted his tin coffee cup, sipped at the coffee, made a disgusted face, and dumped its contents. Cummings had been drinking most of the evening and had been retching and vomiting most of the early morning. Now, white and trembling, he watched his horse being saddled.

"Take Lieutenant Palmer along. Teach him the ropes." Slocum lifted his eyebrows.

"And by that I don't mean for you to continue your disgusting habit of brawling. Do I make myself clear?"

The packers were cursing the mules as they lashed on the packs. The aroma of bacon hung in the still air. Mounts plunged back and forth on their pickets as they performed the ritual show of reluctance. Saddle blankets kept slipping off; troopers cursed, but not as violently as the packers, who could only keep their patience with refractory mules by embarking upon the wildest flights of obscene imagination in which they mentioned, at length, the ancestry of each animal. It was the usual morning scene of a cavalry command on the march. Slocum rather liked it.

He turned back to Horton. "Yes, sir," he said.

There was something in the man's face, thought Horton, that made him uneasy. He couldn't quite place his finger on it, but it annoyed and angered him. For a man like Horton, the only way to control men like this Snow—who, after all, was not dependent upon Horton's good graces for promotion, since he came from a different unit—was to make life difficult for him.

There was no way that Horton could have guessed why Slocum looked at him like that. And the reason was simple— after all, Slocum was not a member of the regular army. And what made it even more hilarious, as far as Slocum was concerned, was that he had once been an officer in the Confederate cavalry. It was a farce, and Slocum was beginning to enjoy it.

"I'll need an experienced scout, sir," he told the colonel now.

"I told you to teach the lieutenant the ropes. He'll only learn by experience."

"Yes, sir, but the country ahead looks pretty bad. I'd prefer a sharper pair of eyes."

"What the hell can you do about it?" Horton demanded.

"I'd like the Apache."

"For God's sake, man, he's only got *one* eye!"

"Yes, sir. I'd still like him," Slocum said.

"Take the red bastard. And don't get yourself into a mess, like you did with Cummings leading the other day."

"Yes, sir," Slocum said. He believed in spraying "sirs" everywhere whenever possible. It did no harm.

Horton grunted and walked away.

Late that afternoon Slocum held up his hand. Palmer and Eskiminzin halted. Slocum had taken the lead when it had become clear that Eskiminzin's eye socket was paining him so much that he could not concentrate on scanning the countryside. But Apaches did not believe that a minor problem like one eye should prevent a man from doing his job. They had been following a pleasant, grassy valley, when suddenly they began to see exhausted horses. Near the mouth of a box canyon which was so damp from water trickling down the rock face that ferns clung to the walls they came upon fifteen horses.

"What do you think?" Palmer asked.

"Indians put 'em here to recuperate." At Eskiminzin's puzzled expression at the last word, Slocum amended it. "Rest up."

They had been ridden hard. Some were Indian ponies, some had the U.S. brand still on them, some were pack-horses.

"Yaquis or Apaches?"

" 'paches. Chiricahua," Eskiminzin said.

"How does he know that?" Palmer demanded.

"Moccasin design on the dirt," Slocum said, pointing down.

"With *one* good eye?" Palmer said. He had a faint, half bored arrogance and assurance that Slocum had learned tended to accompany those who had been born in luxury and who had always had deferential servants surrounding them. A man like Slocum, who had come from a hard hill farm, and who made his way to the Confederate cavalry by sheer ability and courage, without a single lift up from influential friends or family, always felt somewhat resentful at the easy path people such as Palmer walked through life.

"With one good eye," Slocum said sharply.

"Move fast, *fast*," Eskiminzin said urgently.

Slocum realized that the Apache was right. With tired horses around there had to be scouts watching. They had no time to waste; they had to find a safe place to stay till dark.

He looked around. The river had cut a shelf under a rock cliff a quarter of a mile to the north. They couldn't be seen from above—assuming that they had not yet been spotted—and if they were attacked it would be a good place to hole up in. Their only hope was that the Apaches were so sure that no one would ever come this way that their guard had been minimal and not as careful as it would have been in U.S. territory, with an aggressive cavalry constantly patrolling. Here in Mexico, with a much more loosely knit army, the Apaches might not be so vigilant.

Palmer didn't move. Eskiminzin, despairing, shoved him.

Palmer flared up. "Take your goddamn—" he began.

Slocum snapped, *"Move,* you dumb son of a bitch!" He leaned forward, grabbed the reins of Palmer's horse, and kicked the animal in the ribs. The horse moved smartly.

All three moved out at a fast trot.

"I won't forget this," Palmer said. His face was flushed.

"Goodness me," Slocum said dryly.

When Palmer reached down for the reins Slocum wrapped them around his right fist. "Behave like a spoiled brat," he said, watching the heights above the cliff for any danger sign, "and I'll treat you like one."

"They'll see our tracks," Palmer said. "Let's get the hell out of here!"

Slocum stared at him. "Listen to me, Palmer," he said. "There's plenty of horse tracks around. Lots of them are from shod horses. If no one's watching us right this second, we might get away with it. If we try to ride out—*adios!* So we'll stay till it gets dark; then we stand a better chance of getting out of this valley. Is that clear?"

The overhanging cliff was big enough so that they could ride right under it. They dismounted and led their horses as far under the overhang as possible. Eskiminzin sat down cross-legged in shadow and scanned the valley slowly from left to right in one long, sweeping gaze. Then his one good eye gazed up and along the ridge opposite. Nothing.

"I—" Palmer began.

"Shut up," Slocum said. His voice was as hard as granite, though he spoke very softly.

"Listen, you—" Palmer raised his voice.

Eskiminzin spun around. Palmer could see the red hole in his head and the single black eye glittering. Then the Apache turned to Slocum, as if waiting for Slocum to speak the words that had to be said.

"Don't you understand?" Slocum whispered. "If anyone there hears us we are *dead*. Don't say a fucking word till I say so. Or, by God, I'll clip you with my gun butt, brother officer or not!"

"But there aren't—" Palmer began. Then he heard what both Eskiminzin and Slocum had heard earlier, with their sharpened senses: the sound of horses' hooves clopping in shallow water around the bend. Eskiminzin's right hand, the biggest right hand Palmer had ever seen, with broken knuckles and crisscrossed with scars, gripped Palmer's right bicep with tremendous power. It was all Palmer could do to keep from crying out with the pain, but he managed to control his automatic shout of complaint.

Slocum hissed in his ear, "Don't move a fraction of an inch, you dumb son of a bitch. You so much as twitch, and we don't stand any more chance than a stump-tailed bull in fly time."

Nine mounted Apaches came into sight, laughing and talking. Palmer, whose acquaintance with Indians was limited to a few scouts and some others he had seen scrounging around the fort, was surprised to see Indians laughing. One rider suddenly shoved another so hard that he fell off his horse and splashed backward into the shallow river. Everyone roared with laughter. Slocum prayed silently that their own horses would refrain from neighing in response to the Indians' horses. That was sure to attract attention.

And a scout's function was never to attract attention, but to acquire intelligence of the enemy without the enemy's knowledge.

Palmer stared, fascinated, at the dirty white breechclouts and the knee-high deerskin boots the Indians wore. Bandoliers of cartridges crossed their brown chests. Their crow-black, shiny hair hung free down to their shoulders. They all had a massive chest build, with big back and shoulder muscles. The bandoliers, Slocum noted, were all full of cartridges. They must have been doing well, either getting them by raids or by trading.

Four of the men had carbines shoved into their saddle scabbards which looked suspiciously like U.S. cavalry issue. The man who had been pushed into the water remounted, shaking his fist in a mocking way at the one who had done the shoving. The others laughed, then they moved on. When they had disappeared around the bend of the river, Slocum let out a long breath.

Eskiminzin said, "They been doin' purty good."

Slocum nodded.

The Apache said, "They feelin' purty slick, I reckon."

"What's he mean?" Palmer demanded.

"They had a successful raid," Slocum said. "No signs of mourning, so no one was killed. They feel very safe here, that's clear. They probably are keeping a very light guard."

"What now?" Palmer demanded.

"We wait. We just wait here and we don't move till dark, friend Palmer."

"See here, Snow, I've had just about all I care to take from you! My rank is lieutenant, and don't you forget it—"

"You shit up, shavetail bastard!" Eskiminzin hissed.

It was all Slocum could do to refrain from laughing aloud at the Apache's unintentional pronunciation. Palmer reddened, but even he had sense enough not to make an issue of it right then.

It was three hours till dark. Slocum thought the sun would never go down. When he had gone to Sunday school back in West Virginia, he had doubted the Bible teacher's assertion that the sun had stood still for Joshua's battle. But after that afternoon down in Mexico he never doubted that the sun could stand still again.

When it was dark they moved out slowly. Eskiminzin took the lead, as his hearing was uncanny. Slocum followed right behind, since his two good eyes would have to make up for Eskiminzin's missing one.

"Why are we moving so slow?" Palmer demanded in that querulous, half whining, half arrogant tone Slocum had come to hate.

Slocum replied shortly, "We have to move at the pace of a grazing horse. A fast trotting or fast walking horse means he's carrying a rider. Clear?"

Palmer grunted.

Slocum thought, *What an insolent puppy! No wonder Cummings hates the arrogant shit.* Then he thought of Eskiminzin's unwitting error in telling Palmer to "shit up," and that made him chuckle aloud.

"What's so funny?" Palmer demanded. Slocum shook his head. After all, it was important to be fair, and Palmer had never been in battle, and had no idea of the amusing things that could emerge from the horror of combat. Slocum remembered a battle early in sixty-two when a Yankee cannonball bounced toward the rebel lines and a soldier stood up and pretended to kick it as it went by. It took his leg off at the hip and Slocum still thought of the way their laughter changed to silent awe as the man bled to death with a puzzled look that this serious thing had happened to him when all he had wanted to do was make a little joke.

Along the far side of the river small fires glowed in the darkness. Figures passed back and forth in front of the fires. Eskiminzin began to count. When he had finished he jogged Slocum's elbow. They walked slowly, leading the horses. Eskiminzin looked warily for the horse guard. He would take great pleasure in killing him with a knife thrust into the belly, an upward rip, then a quick withdrawal, and the next—and final—slash across the throat.

There was no guard. Eskiminzin frowned in disappointment. But the function of a scouting patrol was to bring back information, not to let itself be lured into combat, no matter how delicious a temptation it might be.

They did not run across any Apaches all the way out of the valley. Palmer's distaste for Slocum was so strong that Slocum almost felt it coming at him in waves. The puppy's dislike only served to amuse Slocum now that the danger was past. Once, in the starlight, Palmer caught Slocum's amused smile, and he grew even more bitter and sullen. Eskiminzin caught the subtle byplay. He did not like it. This hostility could only result in disaster. Officers should not hate each other; in battle such contrary behavior could only result in commands that were refused or argued about, or complied with slowly and reluctantly. And all these were avenues to death.

They mounted and moved back toward the command at a fast trot, except when a mountain trail had to be navigated. The drops were dizzying; Slocum and Eskiminzin let the reins slacken and trusted to the night vision of their horses. Palmer, unused to mountain trails, especially at night, kept his horse on such a short rein that the horse became jittery and almost plunged over a couple of times.

"Slacken off," Slocum said gently at one critical point.

But Palmer burst out with, "For the love of God, are you going to tell me how to *ride?*"

That was enough for Slocum. His patience had limits. But the trail broadened, and there was no danger any more. Still, he felt that the young man had yelled too loudly in a country where a man's voice could carry long distances to anyone who might be listening for strange sounds. It was clear that Palmer's feelings of hostility took precedence over the kind of caution that should be second nature to an officer on a scouting expedition. If he were asked again to go on a scout with Palmer, Slocum would refuse. And, if pressed, he would give his reasons. It was difficult enough risking his life in Apache country under an assumed identity without having to rely for support on an arrogant fool who refused to learn from his mistakes. Slocum had made plenty of mistakes in his years as a cavalryman, but never the same one twice. This young man ran along in his rigid ways like a stubborn locomotive headed for a washed-out bridge, unable—or more likely, thought Slocum, unwilling—to slam on the brakes.

He shrugged. Each man makes his own fate. Slocum had chosen his; Palmer had chosen his, and each of them would have to bear the consequences no matter how bad they were. Slocum would give Palmer no more advice.

Palmer had fallen back. He was very well aware how much Slocum and the Apache disliked him, and by withdrawing he showed his lack of concern.

Eskiminzin suddenly spoke, with a jerk of his chin toward the lieutenant. "He think he a *tigre*."

"A jaguar?" Slocum turned and stared at Eskiminzin.

"And you is a burro. He thinks, that man."

"You mean I'm stubborn?"

"No, no." Eskiminzin spoke impatiently. He asked Slocum if he had seen a fight between a burro and a jaguar. Slocum had seen many things, but that he had never seen.

The night was cool. There were night sounds—crickets, birds in the occasional grove of trees, the sound of a little waterfall formed where a spring came out of a precipice.

"When a *tigre* lands on a burro's back," Eskiminzin said in Apache, "it thinks all is over for the burro. Horses give up right away. But a burro brings up its two back hooves and sinks them into the *tigre's* belly. Frequently it rips open the belly, and the *tigre* either lets go and dies, or it hangs on and dies for sure.''

Slocum felt flattered at the comparison.

''How far, do you say?'' asked Horton. His air of boredom had slipped away.

''Maybe thirty miles. Southeast. Bad trails. Plenty water. Plenty grass.''

Horton grunted. Slocum was slouched against the back of Horton's folding camp chair. It was not the position that Horton approved of in a junior officer, but he realized that Slocum didn't give a damn. Strange, Horton thought. *The man doesn't care about a bad report from me. Which he can be damn sure he'll get!*

The sun was up an hour. Slocum had ridden up as soon as he came in. Eskiminzin was sitting cross-legged on the ground, eating beans with a tablespoon. The tent flap faced east, and the three men were warmed by the rising sun. It had been a chilly night and dew was still clinging in perfect round diamond drops to the grass stems. A flock of tiny brilliant green parrots flew over, squawking violently, on their way to eat cactus fruit somewhere on the lower slopes.

Slocum yawned. He had not slept the night before. Horton's face darkened with anger. What bad manners to place before a superior officer! Palmer obviously shared Horton's feelings about etiquette.

''How many?'' Horton asked.

''Two hundred, two hundred and fifty.''

''Couldn't you be more precise?''

''No, sir. We counted 'em at night. Didn't want to be around by daylight.''

''Nervous?''

''You bet,'' Slocum said placidly. Then he added, ''Sir,'' with a smile that Horton found enraging. *Another thing in my report,* Horton thought. *Insolence.* The thought that the report would really rake Snow over the coals and quite possibly ruin any chance he had for promotion put Horton into a better mood, and he smiled in return. This puzzled Palmer, who could not understand Horton's sudden good humor in the face of such obvious insolence.

"How long d'you think they've been holed up there?"

"Eskiminzin and I figure about a week. Plenty of deer sign up there. He thinks they're resting from various war parties here and there. So they're filling up their bellies and having a high old time for themselves. We didn't see any scouts out."

"Not like them at all," Horton said slowly.

"Nope. But they've never been attacked up there before, Eskiminzin says. The Mexicans don't dare come at 'em so high up, away from the roads. Too easy to be ambushed."

"Ah," Horton said slowly. "Two hundred and fifty!" He seemed impressed. That number of Apaches in one group was a great many, so far as Apaches were concerned.

Slocum looked at him with irony. He was sure that the colonel was, in his imagination, reading the headlines back home: TWO HUNDRED AND FIFTY VICIOUS APACHES SLAIN BY WAR HERO COLONEL ISRAEL HORTON IN GREAT BATTLE AFTER PERILOUS MARCH DEEP INTO THEIR STRONGHOLD.

"Come in, Cummings!" Horton exclaimed. "Good news!"

Cummings walked in. He nodded in a friendly and abstracted manner at Slocum. Eskiminzin lifted his spoon in salute from his beans. Palmer looked disgusted as if he were wishing that Indians did not have to be used for scouting.

Then Cummings noticed Eskiminzin's one good eye. "My God," he said.

Eskiminzin shrugged, then smiled. "One dead Meskin," he said and dismissed the whole subject. It was clear that he wanted Cummings to drop any talk about it.

"Well, Cummings," Horton said exuberantly, rubbing his palms together in a satisfied manner, "we've got the bastards at last. Put out plenty of men as flankers tomorrow. If they spot anyone who might see us, I want every effort made to take 'em prisoner. No shooting, no bugle for reveille. The sergeants will wake everyone. No fires today or tonight. We'll camp close enough to 'em for a dawn attack. One hundred rounds for each man. Lieutenant Palmer, you will follow with the pack train. One troop to guard it. You will make as much speed as you can, but if you fall behind, do not try to catch up. I don't want the mules ruined. Any questions?"

He stood up and lit a cigar. As usual, he was impeccably dressed. Cummings looked with a mixture of distaste and admiration at the colonel's neatness; it almost verged on dandyism.

Slocum saw the play of expression on Cummings's face. Slocum turned and looked at Palmer. The young man clearly didn't like the idea of being in charge of something so lacking in flair as a pack mule train plugging along in the dust of a cavalry command, but he managed to keep his face impassive. Slocum repressed a grin: he had suffered the same anguish in the early months of the War, but he got over it quickly one afternoon outside Shiloh when his train was suddenly jumped by a bluebelly patrol that had let the bulk of the regiment ride by, since they were seeking an easy target. Every since that afternoon Slocum was never bored at being handed charge of a pack train.

"Oh, we'll get them, we'll get them!" Horton exclaimed suddenly. "By God, we'll get 'em!" He turned to Cummings, and said, suddenly friendly, "Eh, Cummings?"

Slocum watched Cummings's face. The captain had a cigar, and his hat sat squarely upon his head. His cigar stuck straight out. Slocum thought with some amusement that the man's posture and expression was very much like General Grant's.

Cummings slowly took his cigar out of his mouth and looked at it. It had gone out. He gravely lit another match and applied it with care to the ragged end. It was a cheap cigar, not like Horton's Havanas, and Horton tried to conceal a look of distaste while Cummings went through his manipulations. When he had at last got it going to his satisfaction he took a deep breath.

"No questions," he said.

Horton let out a long, irritated sigh. "Well, then, get plenty of rest."

The officers filed out. Some of them stood talking quietly near the tent. As Slocum walked out he passed by Rigby, who was talking to a fat corporal about his favorite subject, the colonel.

"I been with 'im since 'bout the time he left the Point," he was saying. Slocum slowed his pace in order to listen. "He ain't much at talkin'," the orderly went on, "but I tell you he's a whale at fightin'! You ought to've seen him at Little Bluffs. Our company was layin' behind a fence, an' a reb battery was jus' givin' us fits. A good many o' the boys got it through the head; an' then at last Cap'n Thomas went down. A sergeant seen him drop an' he run across an' told the lieutenant—that's the colonel now. 'Lieutenant,' he says, 'the cap'n's killed an' that battery's knockin' hell outa the company. Ain't it 'most time to get a move on?' "

Rigby paused for maximum effect. Slocum slowed to hear the rest. Cummings had managed to relight his stubborn cigar and was walking toward Slocum. Both of them heard Rigby continue, " 'Why, cert'nly,' says the lieutenant, 'let's go a little closer.' "

Cummings caught up with Slocum. "That's a lovely story," he said, jerking his head toward the proud Rigby. "A very lovely story. That'll make the *Indianapolis Star*, no fear. But I know another story about him, one which will never appear in any campaign biography. Want to hear it?''

''Sure,'' Slocum said.

They began strolling toward their tent. Sergeants were shouting commands, corporals passed them on, and the apparent mad confusion of a cavalry command preparing to break camp and move on was everywhere about them. Cummings's eyes darted all around, and he saw that things were going well and would not be improved by any orders from him. Palmer was bustling about with an important air. He left a trail of sly grins behind him from the men, who knew their business.

''I was with General Phipps's division. Did you know Phipps?''

Indeed, Slocum knew Phipps. Slocum had been sitting in the branches of an oak alongside the Tennessee River one night while Phipps was writing on his traveling desk by candlelight. Slocum trained a squirrel rifle on his heart from the tree. Phipps was in the stateroom of a riverboat, and Slocum was a sniper then. He had been ordered to kill all the higher Union officers he found. But he simply could not do it; he could not shoot an unarmed man who was very likely writing a letter to his wife. Logically, he should have done it, of course—the death of a high officer would certainly be a setback for any army, particularly a fine officer such as General Phipps.

But Slocum slowly let his hammer down. Later that night he came out of the tree and reported to his superiors. He quietly told them that if he were asked to perform any more sniping duties, he would simply desert. His officers knew they had exceptional material in Slocum and relented.

''No,'' Slocum said. ''No, I never met Phipps.''

Palmer joined them. Cummings grunted in response to Palmer's curt nod at the two men.

''I was with Phipps's division,'' Cummings went on. The cigar stuck out from his mouth at an upward angle.

His hands were deep in his pockets. Slocum's hands were thrust into his back pockets. The air was a little chilly.

"We rode into some town or other, Hendersonville or Robertsville, something like that. Our respected colonel here had become a brigadier general by then. I think it was early in sixty-four."

Palmer had tensed at the remark about Horton. Cummings paid no attention and went calmly on. "Horton had made his headquarters in one of the better houses. It was plantation country, cotton and indigo. When I got there a little girl was having convulsions. She had been in the bathtub when a bunch of stragglers burst into the house. They took all of the meat and all of the provisions they could find. All the time this was going on, the colonel kept sitting in the dining room. The woman who owned the house found a silver teaspoon on the floor. It had fallen from the pocket of one of Horton's men. She took it it to Horton and asked him with a straight face if he had dropped it. He didn't like that much. He considered himself insulted."

"Well, by God, he had a right—" Lieutenant Palmer began.

"You think so, eh?" Cummings asked softly. "I remember old Phipps, who would not take a private house for himself, and who fretted over the theft of a sweet potato."

"Damn rebs!" Palmer burst out. "I wish I had been in the War! I wish I could have had the whole Southern Confederacy hanging over hell on a thin rope, and I would take my knife and . . ." he made a vicious slicing gesture with his hand.

"Funny," said Slocum, watching Palmer. "No one I knew at the Point who fought in the War ever talked like that."

Cummings grinned. Palmer flushed as he looked from one captain to the other. He did not understand them.

"I—" he began.

"You're outnumbered, sonny," Slocum said. "Run along and play."

Cummings burst into a roar of laughter as Palmer stormed away.

"Trouble ahead with that one," Slocum said. "He's like a little kitten that keeps scratching you and scratching you and won't stop even when you give it a little tap on the nose. Eventually you have to give it a real whop."

8

Palmer had his men packed and on the march by the time the command was cooking breakfast. When the command broke camp they would be three miles ahead. That added distance would give them time to get into the night camp while it was still light.

As Slocum and Cummings rode, the captain asked Slocum if he had ever been to the Dakotas. Slocum's policy was to keep everything about his past and his travels a secret from everyone, even people he liked, as he did Cummings.

"No," Slocum said.

"Those Dakotas up there don't behave like the Apaches," Cummings remarked, watching the flankers scrabbling on the harsh slopes abutting the trail. Occasionally a horse would lose its footing and slide down a bit in a shower of stones, dust, and muttered curses. Horton's warning to keep quiet had struck fear into the men. They understood the fighting qualities of the Apaches very well. They moved with the signs of tension visible in their faces and their bearing.

"Whenever they came into the sutler's store at one of the posts they behaved all right. But if you met them outside," Cummings went on with a shrug, "they wouldn't speak to you, even if they knew you. They all covered up their heads and faces with their blankets except for one eye they peeked at you with. It made you feel mighty queer when you knew there were thousands of 'em within thirty miles and you out on a patrol with maybe fifteen or twenty men. Brrr!'' he shivered at the memory.

The country they were traveling had been picked clean by the Apaches and by the endless revolutions. The few haciendas they passed were like fortresses. They had thick walls with slits for rifles and they all had lookout towers with huge bells which could be rung in case of attack. The smaller ranches had been abandoned. At noon they came to Jarral Grande, a sprawling pueblo set in the chaparral typical of the lower reaches of the mountains. On the outskirts was a cemetery filled with white crosses which had faded to a misty gray. Most of the houses had been burned. In one a rabbit sat on the threshold. The gardens still had flowers, but they were choked with weeds. A big white cat crept under a melon vine and would not respond to Cummings's entreaty for it to emerge and be petted and fed.

The Apaches had torn off the roof of the pueblo, and from its upper walls they had shot arrows down at the dwellers. Inside was the skeleton of a dog and a mass of human bones which had been gnawed by rats and coyotes. There was no sound in the pueblo except the croaking of a bullfrog from a spring in a nearby arroyo.

The soldiers were uneasy. They watered their horses and got under way as quickly as possible.

An hour later they reached the first slopes of the foothills that led up to the mountains. Now was the time to be eternally vigilant and to move with extraordinary caution. Cummings halted his company and made every man remove the cartridges in his weapons lest someone should fire by accident and alert the whole mountain range.

Chaparral began to give way to pitahaya and Spanish bayonet. The wind grew stronger. They came to a little spring with a few old willows hanging over it. A flight of tiny green parrots flew out of the trees, all chattering at once. Cummings grinned and said it sounded like kids being let out of school after a long day. At the spring they found moccasin footprints and many hoofprints. The prints went in the same direction they were going.

Cummings fell silent when he saw them. Slocum dismounted, knelt above the footprints, and bent down. He straightened up and dusted his knees. "All safe," he said. "Several hours old."

"How the hell do you know?" Palmer asked. The mule train had made extraordinarily good time, and he had come up to the company while they had watered. But the young man's tone, Slocum decided, was not too overbearing.

"Well, you see," Slocum said, "the wind's been blowing from the southwest all morning. Last night's dew kept the dirt a bit damp. So the sides of the prints were sharp—real sharp—right after sunrise. Then the wind began to blow. As the dirt dried, the wind began to move it. The sharp sides started to crumble a bit, and more and more grains fell into the hole. So I figure they'd been here four, five hours ago."

"Umm," Palmer said grudgingly. He turned and walked off.

"Gracious little prick, isn't he?" said Slocum, amused.

"He's got a long way to go," Cummings said. "And he may never get there."

"Oh, come on," Slocum said indulgently. "We were all young and stupid once."

"Yes, I grant you that," Cummings replied. "But not vicious."

The foothills were higher and the contour lines began to move closer together. They came upon canyons, some of them with sides that rose straight up for two thousand feet. Wherever a river ran along the bottom of a canyon, masses of ferns had managed to secure a foothold on the rock face, and Slocum thought it was like passing through a greenhouse full of hanging plants. Hummingbirds flicked through the air like multicolored tiny firecrackers. The hum of the bees seemed very loud since the men had received their instructions to talk no louder than a quiet conversational tone. Singing was forbidden. After the sun had passed the zenith it seemed like twilight in each canyon—very much, Slocum thought, like the redwood groves he had passed through in the High Sierra, where there were only twenty minutes of sun each day, and that when the sun was directly overhead. The air seemed soft and drenched in peace; it was almost impossible to believe that so much blood had been spilled in the Sierra Madre, ever since the first Spanish conquistadors had come along this way with their steel cuirasses and awkward muskets, sweating in their armor and afflicted mightily with illness. Intestinal disorders could make a man mighty unfriendly, and so the Spaniards began their reign of terror for which they were beginning to reap the long delayed reaction.

After threading his way down one of the steep trails, Slocum looked up. He could see the mules of Palmer's pack train; they looked no larger than mice. They grew to the size of rats as they moved downwards, then they became dog-size.

One mule was pushed off the trail by another one crowding against him. He was mashed to a pulp by his impact on the rocks below. The remaining mules descended without incident. Slocum moved along the canyon floor with the uneasy feeling that great boulders might crash down on them should the Apaches have been alerted to their presence in the mountains. The usual laughing and jostling ceased as the packers cursed the mules forward with quiet desperation so they could get through the narrow, dangerous canyon as quickly as possible.

Suddenly there came a crash of thunder. Luckily for them, they had come out of the canyon. The sky turned black within three minutes, and the air was filled with such heavy rain that visibility was only a few feet. Entire mountainsides were covered with sheets of water inches deep. Arroyos filled up and walls of dirty brown water roared between the narrow rock walls.

It ended as quickly as it had begun. Within five minutes the air was steaming as the ground dried up and the water sank into the sandy beds of the arroyos.

That night no fires were permitted. They ate cold beef and drank from a small, icy creek filled with clear green water. No one slept well that night except Slocum, who had learned from experience that when any sleep could be had he had better grab it. The extra margin of strength a man could have when he had rested and eaten decently could very well mean the difference between living and dying should a critical encounter develop.

He left with Eskiminzin on a scout. Four miles in front of the command they found a band of fifteen ponies which had been driven into a small box canyon.

Slocum rolled over on his back and stared at the brilliant turquoise sky. A few huge, billowing white clouds like fairy-tale castles moved slowly, pushed gently by a west wind. They were lying just below the crest of the ridge above the canyon. Slocum yawned. He could have used more sleep.

Eskiminzin said, "What you think?" Slocum grinned. Eskiminzin was always trying to test him. The wind pushed at his hair; Slocum had taken off his hat to dry off the sweat that the climb on foot from the valley below had produced.

"Resting," Slocum said, "just like the horses the other day."

Eskiminzon grunted. That meant he agreed.

"How long they been there?" the Apache demanded.

"Not long."

"How you know?"

"Grass doesn't look cropped much," said Slocum.

Eskiminzin grunted in satisfaction. "You right."

They slid down the hill until they could stand upright, then they rode back quickly.

Colonel Horton listened to their report.

"I say they've been left there by a war party which had split in two. Let's go after the other half. Lieutenant Palmer, take three platoons and go find 'em. The rest of the command will go forward. Cummings, you'll take the pack train. Clear?"

Cummings folded his arms. It was very clear. In fact, it was transparent. Palmer was to have a good chance at acquiring some glory when he found the war party. With luck he'd be mentioned in dispatches and might be promoted. Cummings would get the dirty work, miss all the action, and wind up still a captain even after this spectacular victory. He caught Slocum looking at him, flushed, and dropped his eyes. It was his duty to follow with the pack train. He said nothing, and passed Palmer as that triumphantly smiling young man mounted in front of his three platoons. The men looked at Cummings disconsolately. They preferred the experienced captain, but were smart enough to keep their discontent suppressed. Palmer was the Colonel's fair-haired boy, and they knew it.

Palmer rode off, veering to the right. Horton then led off with the bulk of the command. Slocum led a company. They moved forward down a narrow canyon. The country's speciality seemed to be narrow canyons, Slocum thought grimly. Talking was forbidden. A very experienced officer would have made sure that the iron-shod hooves of the horses had been muffled with anything, even the men's shirts, but Horton didn't order it, and Slocum knew that any suggestion coming from him would be disregarded.

Behind them Cummings's pack train moved. A turn in the trail cut the command from his sight. Three minutes later there came several crashing volleys of the carbines.

Cummings halted. He had the mules unpacked as fast as the packers could manage it. He made them pile up the loads to form a breastwork. He stretched a picket line, tied the mules to it, left four men behind as a guard, and rode hard toward the firing with the rest.

As he rounded the bend in the trail, pounding along at a full gallop, Horton saw a vertical cliff eight hundred feet high. Twenty feet above the valley floor the cliff seemed to have slid back to form a shelf, shaped to make a shallow cave. Great blocks of stone which had fallen in some long-ago cataclysm made a natural breastwork. The only way up or down was via long ladders, which had been pulled up by the Apaches. The ends of the ladders stuck out a few feet over the edge of the cliff. To Slocum the arrangement looked very much like the pueblo dwellings up the Rio Grande valley; they had the same system of defense via the ladder technique.

Horton had halted the command. Cummings thought the colonel had made a pretty good disposition. Half the men formed a skirmish line behind the boulders, which were scattered over the valley floor below the cave. The remaining men he had placed in reserve fifty yards behind the skirmish line. Each man had placed a handful of cartridges on the rock behind which he happened to be lying.

Cummings placed his men in the reserve line. Then he crawled behind the rocks, taking advantage of their excellent natural cover, till he reached Horton.

The colonel was on one knee. He beckoned Slocum to him. Above the rattling roar of the carbines Horton asked, "These the Apaches you saw?"

Slocum shook his head. "No," he said. "They're about fifteen miles further on."

"Doesn't matter," Horton said happily. "There's plenty for me up there!"

Eskiminzin crawled close to Slocum. "They musta been dancin'," he said. "Drinkin'. No scouts, no lookouts neither.'' As long as he could remember, Eskiminzin added, the Apaches had never been chased this far into the Sierra Madre. He did not know this cave.

Behind the boulders up on the cliff, the Apaches could not see the soldiers. Anyone putting his head to one side for a look was as good as dead, with the massive firepower the soldiers commanded. But they had plenty of arrows and lances. Slocum saw a dead gray horse. A few feet farther on he saw a dead trooper feathered with arrows.

"Keep your heads down!" Slocum said sharply. "You show your head anywhere and sizzle come the bullets at it!"

For a while the Apaches tried the old trick of poking a hat on a stick from behind one of the rocks to tempt the troopers to expose themselves for a shot, but Horton and Cummings kept the men from responding. Someone poked Slocum from the rear and mumbled, "Cap'n, Cap'n," and Slocum, not turning around, said abruptly, "Later, later." But the man kept prodding him until Slocum turned.

An arrow had gone clean through the man's neck. Blood dripped from the arrowhead and the tiny bunched-up feathers seemed to sprout on the other side like a gray carrot top. The arrow had passed between his windpipe and the vertebrae. As a medical orderly sawed away at the arrow shaft the trooper lifted his head in spite of the remonstrances of the orderly not to move. He glared at the other troopers, who were staring at him in fascinated wonder. Finally he demanded, "What the hell you gapin' at, you danged fools? Didn't you ever see an arrow before?"

After he was bandaged Slocum sent him on his hands and knees to rest behind a boulder. He spat a little blood, but he would probably recover nicely.

Horton's orders came down the line: skirmish line to fire against the roof of the cave. He hoped that the ricochets would do damage, since there was no way to inflict damage on the Apaches in that almost impregnable position.

The men were to fire at will and continuously. After two rounds had been fired, Horton smiled. A child had begun screaming inside the cave.

Next Slocum heard yells of defiance.

"Cease firing!" Horton ordered. The firing became ragged, then stopped. He beckoned Eskiminzin close. "Tell 'em to send the women and kids out."

Slocum grunted and looked at Cummings, who rolled over closer and said, with his ironic smile, "The eyes of the republic are on him."

The Apaches refused to send anyone out. They screamed and cursed at the attackers.

"Commence firing," Horton said, in a mechanical tone, as if he were on the practice range back at the fort.

The monotonous crash of the firing continued, coupled more and more often with the screams of wounded women and children.

Horton didn't like it. He frowned. If he killed too many non-combatants, the whole affair would look bad on his record. "Cease firing!" he snapped. He jerked his head at Eskiminzin. The scout wriggled closer to the cave, taking advantage of every dip in the terrain. He cupped his huge hands to his mouth and lifted his mahogany-colored face with the red cavity where his eye had been. He trumpeted another demand that they surrender in the harsh, hissing Apache tongue.

There was no answer. Slocum had known there wouldn't be. Apaches simply did not surrender. A chant began in the cave. Slocum looked at the ground in front of his face in silent despair. He knew what the chant meant, and there was nothing he could do about it.

Eskiminzin said, "Colonel, that there's their death song. They're gonna come out fast. You better watch out."

"Pass the word!" Cummings yelled to the troopers on his right and left flanks. "They're going to charge!"

On both sides he heard the message being repeated. One

trooper began to tremble. A corporal shouted, "What's this? Jesus, Mary, an' Joseph, Holy Moses, he would be a sojer!"

Horton, with his keen hearing, caught the catcall. "Trooper!" he called out sharply.

"Yes, sir!" said the trembling man.

"Your first action?"

The man stammered out a nervous assent.

"I was just as scared as you my first time, son," Horton said. "Probably worse. When the time comes I know you won't disgrace me." He was trying to be kind.

Cummings turned and grinned with absolute delight. "Every move that Gila monster makes is calculated. And this time he outdid himself. The trooper who won't disgrace him is the worst man in my company. I bet he'll just put his head down and shit in his pants. Mark my words, Snow. And when the time comes for Horton to relate today's wonders, I'll bet you this little incident will be described as one in which he inspired that nauseating coward to feats of courage, thus marking the colonel as a man who could lead this country to amazing feats of glory—"

"Jesus!" Slocum interrupted, staring up at the cliff.

Cummings pivoted on his belly. He saw thirty warriors, each with a quiver full of arrows slung across his back, a bow slung from the opposite shoulder, and a carbine in his hands, suddenly appear between the rocks at the cliff edge. Several ladders were run out from the cave and lowered into position. The men scrambled down, as sure-footed as mountain goats, and then charged, screaming and firing their carbines as they ran.

Cummings's prediction was borne out. Horton's brave little trooper screamed and ran to the rear as fast as he could go. The sergeants were so startled by the surprise attack that none of them stopped the hysterical trooper as he ran and stumbled for safety.

The concentrated blast of the cavalry fire cut the warriors down before they had run fifty yards. The ones who were still alive and able to move tried to crawl back. Four more ragged volleys finished off the remnants of the suicide charge. They dug into the sand with their fingers as their bodies shuddered under the hammer blows of the heavy bullets.

But one of the Apaches had managed to penetrate the skirmish line. He climbed atop a boulder with the agility of a goat. Unaware of the reserve line, which by then had leveled more than a hundred carbines at him, he shook his own carbine at the first skirmish line and yelled defiance. Then he turned, having proven his bravery, and now ready to jump down and make his escape.

For the first time he saw the forest of muzzles pointed at him. He held up his hands in supplication and cried out, *"No, no, soldados!"* He was almost blown to bits by the impact of the bullets.

The firing began again. It was all aimed at the cave roof. A little Apache boy of four ran out and stood at the edge. He was furious. He stood motionless, sucking his thumb. A ricochet seared the side of his head. He began to scream. His mother ran out and pulled him inside, kicking and screaming his rage.

There was no wood to make ladders.

"Keep the ricochets going!" Horton yelled. "They'll surrender soon enough."

One of the men suddenly yelled, "Look out!" and pointed up. Falling toward the outthrust lip of the cave from the edge of the cliff eight hundred feet above, was a tremendous boulder the size of a flour barrel. It hit another boulder which was being used as part of the barricade, and splintered it. Rock fragments flew like bullets. Then the huge boulder bounced backward into the cave with a penetrating clatter. Before it had teetered to a halt, another boulder was falling down from the cliff top.

Lieutenant Palmer had arrived.

He had heard the firing. Leaning over the cliff, he saw what was going on below. The top of the mesa was covered with boulders. Fifty-pounders, hundred-pounders, three-hundred-pounders went rolling over the edge and dropped into the cave. The air in the cave was full of rock dust and chipped and fragmented rock. The screaming sickened Cummings and Slocum and most of the other men. No one came out to surrender. In twenty minutes Horton signaled to Palmer to stop.

No sound came from the cave.

Horton stood up and jerked his chin at Eskiminzin. The Apache stood and called out in Apache, "Do you surrender?"

There was no response.

Slocum stood up and nodded toward the cave as soon as Horton turned to glance at him.

"Go ahead," Horton said.

Slocum took a rope and walked to the cliff. On his second try, he managed to lasso a pointed boulder. He went up easily, hand over hand. Cummings sighed and wished he possessed that agility. Once on the lip of the cave, Slocum took out his Colt and moved warily into the cave. He coughed in the dust that still hovered in the hot, dark air. The thick smell of blood seeped from the crushed bodies. Slocum saw two tiny splintered legs beneath a two-hundred-pound boulder. His heart raced. He had never made war upon children. This was a very dirty business Horton had embarked upon. And there was no need for it—no need for it at all.

Except for Horton's need for political advancement. The man could not even claim he had done this in the heat of battle. He was a cold-blooded murderer, and Slocum prayed briefly that Horton would die in a particularly unpleasant fashion, preferably at Apache hands. They were very inventive when it came to retribution.

Slocum counted the dead. Horton could chalk up to his glory fourteen men, twelve women, and eight children.

In the rear of the cave was a great pile of arrows made with the local reed. There were stacks of lances. There were also fifty-four carbines, most of them army issue, but very little ammunition. That was the problem with guns and Apaches—ammunition was very hard to get and very expensive. They could never get enough practice. Slocum always preferred to meet an Apache with a gun for that reason. With arrows they were deadly up to seventy-five feet.

There were baskets of roasted mescal, jerked mule and horse meat. Horse meat had the advantage that you could ride your butcher shop right to where you wanted it; then you could cut its throat and then proceed to turn it into jerky. And Apaches preferred horse meat to beef any day.

Ollas of water had been ranged against one wall. Now they were all smashed, the water mingled with blood. Two of the children were still alive. Slocum bent over them.

Behind him Cummings, who had climbed more slowly, began to vomit. He straightened up and wiped his lips.

"Know who's going to pay for this?" he asked.

"Sure," Slocum said. "Every white between here and Tucson."

9

"Why don't we just burn it all?" Palmer demanded, looking at the pile of carbines, dried jerky, and blankets piled up on the lip of the cave. "We can't carry all that stuff on the mules."

"It has never ceased to amaze me," Cummings said, "that a pip-squeak lieutenant is always sure that his views on every subject are of deep interest to all." He had recovered, Slocum noted.

"Sergeant!" Cummings ordered. "Break up all the carbines that aren't army issue. Break up all the ollas and dump the mescal."

"Why don't we burn it, like I said?" Palmer persisted.

"You want us to send a telegram to the other band announcing that we're on our way?" Cummings asked with heavy irony. "Jesus Christ, kid, just keep your mouth shut and your bowels open. Maybe you'll learn something."

Palmer flushed. Slocum once more thought that the young man was unusually slow in knowing when to shut up. Any other second lieutenant, stupid though he may have been, would have had sense enough to keep quiet. But Palmer relied on his connection to the colonel to get away with it. He would never learn from experience. If he ever achieved higher rank, Slocum thought, God help the troops he would command.

Palmer went down the ladder. A squad was burying a dead trooper. When they had finished, Horton drove the horses back and forth over the fresh mound in order to destroy all traces of digging.

Eskiminzin looked at him in silence. No Apache would desecrate the grave; they feared the ghosts of the dead would seek them out for revenge. Indeed, when an Apache died in a *jacal* it was immediately burned. The dead Apaches would not be buried.

"Let 'em rot," he said indifferently. When the horses had churned the grave area into a mass of hoofmarks the colonel rose in his stirrups. His spurs had been rubbed very brightly by his orderly. Horton's face showed pride and arrogance as he looked at his command. Then he plunged his closed fist up and down twice. The command moved higher into the Sierra Madre.

Horton sent Slocum and Eskiminzin ahead on a deep scout to look for the *rancheria*. The trail had become so steep and difficult that the pack train moved as quickly as the rest of the command. Horton ordered the pack train to close up. No scouting on either flank was possible in this extremely rough, broken country where almost every line seemed to be vertical. The eye saw only peaks, cliffs, and tortured lava flows which had cooled and then eroded into black basalt arroyos, interlocking with each other in a complex, erratic arrangement that made no pattern and no sense.

Horton's experience had been in the East during the War, mostly in Virginia, where the terrain presented very few difficulties to cavalry maneuvers. His western experience had been in Kansas against the Cheyenne, and in northern Texas against the Comanches. The terrain in both areas was flat, ideal for cavalry.

He was not used to fighting in country like a crazy quilt on end, and he did not like it. As Cummings rode alongside him, he could see Horton frowning at the high cliffs towering above them. Occasionally the trail skirted the edge of a precipice and left the troopers clinging to the rock face like flies on a windowpane. If there should be a sudden volley fired at them they would have as much chance of escaping as a fly would have of escaping a skillfully swung flyswatter. And the worst thing was that the men knew it too.

But there were some things about mountain fighting Cummings knew. He knew, for instance, that if the mountains hid the enemy from the command, they also hid the command from the enemy. He was tempted to remark that if rats popped out of holes in the wall, why not wait patiently by the holes and become rat catchers? But Cummings had reached the point where he would not volunteer any information whatsoever unless he received a direct order first, so he kept quiet.

Behind them the *zapilotes* were already circling slowly above a dead mule which had slipped and broken a foreleg between two rocks. Five minutes after a packer had cut its throat the *zapilotes* had found it. They moved in great circles, slowly lower. They could sail six minutes without a wing flap in the hot air currents rising off the rocky soil.

Cummings looked down at the *zapilotes* from the trail. From that height the vultures looked like fleas. Seeing the mule being picked apart, Palmer turned pale. Cummings told him, "This is not a soft country. Almost everything along the slopes, the bottoms, and the canyons is full of thorns. Every time you break a blade of grass it becomes a thorn at both ends. Take that damn beaver-tail cactus. Looks nice and pretty and soft, doesn't it? Those pink and purple flowers are real nice. I once touched it. Couldn't get the damn spines out for a week."

Palmer was interested, but tried not to show it. Cummings cursed himself for blabbing so much. It was one of his few weaknesses; he had to talk whenever he felt unsure of himself or somewhat nervous. He hoped the command was not moving inexorably into disaster, what with Horton's insane driving ahead. But Cummings hoped that what had been derisively called "Horton's Luck" long ago would still be effective. The man had a facility for putting himself into very sticky messes and then easing himself out of them.

He had been taken down a peg in Colorado for attacking a Cheyenne village in the winter when he had been ordered to go to the relief of another detachment instead.

Company K had been decimated, but Horton had seized a winter's supply of meat and ammunition from a particularly nasty band of hostile Cheyenne. He had wiped out their horses—two hundred thirty of them—and so eliminated the Cheyenne as a hostile force. The result: a slap on the wrist for disobeying orders, three months' suspension without pay— and a mention in dispatches for courage and initiative. Cummings hoped that the man's blind luck would continue.

"Cummings!" the colonel called out.

Cummings rode up to Horton.

"Sir."

Before Horton could say anything it began to rain, another sudden, violent downpour. One of the mules slipped and smashed its load against a rock. Broken signal mirrors and skyrockets were scattered in the mud. Cummings made sure that the rockets would be dried carefully before he moved next to Horton.

"Where the hell are the scouts?" the colonel demanded angrily. "They should have been back by now. Maybe that band left. I want to know what the hell's likely to happen. God damn it all to hell, Cummings, I want some intelligence!"

He rubbed the pommel nervously. Cummings watched him with interest and slight amusement. Horton was unhappy in mountain country, was he? He clearly wanted his hand held; after all, Cummings had more experience fighting Apaches than he did.

Cummings said nothing. There was nothing to say. Obviously, there was no way to contact Snow and Eskiminzin. The rockets might attract their attention if they saw them, but the sight of the rockets would also alert any Apache to the cavalry presence. It was smarter just to wait till the two men returned.

"Cummings, for Christ's sake, answer!"

"Sir," Cummings said soothingly, "there's nothing for us to do except wait."

Rigby stared at him with hot, angry black eyes. Cummings winked at the man, who flushed. Cummings felt nervous, too—any man would get nervous in these mountains. But it did no good to feel nervous, and it was downright dangerous to yield to it. Subordinates would lose confidence and morale would hit the basement. Once in the basement, orders would be misunderstood and sometimes disobeyed, and then it would be a case of every man for himself and the devil take the hindmost.

An officer who became nervous couldn't think fast and accurately. His men would suffer. If he were alone, Cummings thought, he could luxuriate in nervousness all day.

Horton said, surprisingly gently, "I suppose you're right, Cummings. Sorry."

That was one of the things Horton could do once in a while: admit error. It was a very hard thing for him to do. Cummings thought that if things had been different long ago, he and the colonel might well have become good friends. But it was too late now.

Horton pulled off his right glove and gnawed on a knuckle.

"Oh, shit!" he said suddenly, with a disgusted expression.

Ahead, far out of rifle range, he had seen an Apache astride a horse atop a low bluff. The horseman calmly sat for a moment, then disappeared.

"There goes our surprise attack," Horton said morosely. But it was Eskiminzin.

Eskiminzin grinned at Cummings as he rode by. When he passed near Palmer, that young man had just come out from behind a clump of sagebrush where he had gone to relieve himself. One suspender was over a shoulder and the man instinctively dropped the other and dragged out his Colt, but Cummings knocked the barrel up and said contemptuously, "Scout!"

Eskiminzin was not the least bit rattled. He grinned at Palmer. Slocum appeared next. His face was reddened from sunburn. His blue trousers were sodden with sweat and ripped by cactus. To Cummings's raised eyebrows, Slocum nodded. The gesture meant that the Apaches had been located.

Rigby went riding fast down the line. "Colonel's compliments, sir," he said stiffly, "and we camp here, no fires, and will all officers report immediately to the colonel."

When all the officers had gathered around Horton, he burst out in a jubilant tone, "The scouts have found them! We will attack tomorrow at daybreak. They're about ten miles north of here. That right, Captain?"

Slocum nodded.

"Captain Snow will draw a map for you. Captain?"

Slocum squatted. With his palms he cleared the ground, and with a sharpened branch he drew two parallel lines, a foot apart.

"These are the ridges on each side of their valley," he began. "The ridge on the right, the eastern ridge, slopes pretty easily to a wide, sandy beach. Then comes a river about a hundred yards across. Then there's an easy climb out of the river to a flat tableland, well-grassed, with clumps of live oaks scattered here and there. The tableland is about four hundred yards wide. Then come some sand dunes covered with low scrub, sagebrush, and a stony soil between the bushes. These dunes slope upward and then become the western ridge. The *rancheria* is scattered along the edge of the river, on the tableland, under the oaks, and in the grass.''

"How deep is the river?" Horton asked.

"We walked our horses across. Right where we were it's about three feet deep. Elsewhere, I couldn't say.''

"Why didn't you find out?" Palmer demanded. He had taken on the irritating habit of slapping one glove against the other.

Without looking at him, Slocum continued. "My guess is there's from two hundred to two hundred and twenty *jacales* making up the encampment.''

Horton's eyes widened. So did Cummings's. This would make the camp the largest Apache grouping ever recorded.

"Food?" Horton asked. He wondered how such a collection of people could find enough to eat.

"The area is full to bursting with deer, fish, piñon nuts, and mescal. The deer are not in the least bit shy. Obviously they haven't been hunted for years. There was no sign of nervousness when they saw us.''

"Why didn't you check out the depth of the river?" Palmer repeated.

"Oh, Jesus," Cummings muttered.

Slocum turned and looked at Palmer with his narrowed green eyes. He hadn't checked elsewhere up and down the river because the area was full of Apaches dozing here and there, and he could very well have come across a young couple making love. Then the alarm would have been given and the entire encampment would have dispersed like a group of mountain quail into innumerable arroyos, canyons, and mesas, making themselves impossible to run down or to follow.

"I don't like wet socks," Slocum said gently. Someone tittered, and Palmer flushed angrily.

Horton cut it short. "Captain Snow knows what he's

doing, Lieutenant," he said crisply. He put his finger on the ground. "Can I come down this eastern ridge in a fast charge?"

Cummings leaned toward Slocum and whispered in his left ear, "There goes the Young Napoleon again."

Slocum said, "It looks like that might be possible."

"And the river. You don't know how deep it is except in the one place where you crossed?"

"Yes, sir."

"I would like to know more than that about its depth, Captain."

"So would we all, sir," Slocum said courteously.

There was a sudden hush. Horton stiffened. To Cummings it seemed as if Horton's neck had assumed the sinuous curve of a rattlesnake as it reared, ready to strike.

Then he relaxed. "Silly question. I apologize. I had counted on a sudden charge across the river and into that big concentration of *jacales*. But with the depth doubtful it's somewhat risky."

"*Somewhat*, hell!" Cummings burst out. "It's suicide!"

Again there came a stunned hush. Palmer turned and gave the captain a look of unadulterated hatred.

Slocum defused the situation. "We got up on the eastern ridge, sir," he said. "They were hunting deer not far away. We couldn't go any closer and we couldn't stay. Your orders were to come back as soon as we found them."

"Yes," Horton said, suddenly indifferent. It was clear to both Slocum and Cummings that Horton would have dearly loved a traditional cavalry charge. Now that it seemed out of the question his enthusiasm seemed to be waning. "The other ridge, now. Can I charge down it?"

"We couldn't get close enough to see, Colonel," Slocum said. "Maybe. But it was thick-looking scrub. Sagebrush, cholla—that breaks up a charge something fierce."

"I was a brigadier before you entered the Point, Captain."

Slocum broke into a genuinely amused smile at that remark. Horton was not sure what the smile meant; he thought it probably was the new captain's pleasure at hearing a clever remark. Slocum chose to let him think that.

"Captain," Horton went on, "are you sure the plain is grassy along the river? No ravines, no gullies?"

Aha! Slocum thought. *So you're thinking about Custer and the retreat up to the ridge in the Dakotas? Those little gullies where the Cheyenne and the Sioux crept up and surrounded him?*

"Yes, sir," Slocum said. There was to be no Little Bighorn here if Horton could help it. That was somewhat encouraging.

Custer's base had been the riverboat *Far West* two days' march north of him. But Horton's base was much further away.

And Custer had disobeyed orders and gone off, thinking he could pull off a victory over some disorganized redskins. He didn't know he was about to face the largest assembly of armed and hostile Indians in the history of the United States.

Horton, on the other hand, was in complete charge of his unit. He did not have the need to prove himself again and again, the way Custer did. Slocum had no doubt that Horton was pretty damn sure that if Custer had survived— and won at the Little Bighorn—he would have run for senator, governor, or president. All of the bastards wanted to kill a lot of people and then run for office. Slocum smiled in disgust.

"What's so funny, Captain? Do you find me amusing?" the colonel asked.

This was not the time or the place for a confrontation. "No, sir," Slocum said. "A private joke, sir."

Horton took two deep breaths. Then he snapped, "Where do they keep their horses?"

"Here," Slocum said. He squatted. "They're penned in a small box canyon that goes deep into the western ridge here. Maybe three hundred, three hundred and five."

"How the hell can you be so precise, Captain?"

Slocum took a breath, held it, and released it. He did not like being challenged in such a peremptory tone. He knew very well how to count cattle or horses. Years of experience stealing both of them and the need for accurate counts had given him the skill. He could ride slowly around a large horse herd and come up with a count that would be not more than two or three head off.

"Three hunnert three," Eskiminzin said. The words dropped like stones into a pool.

"That takes care of that," Cummings muttered.

There was an embarrassed silence from the other officers. Horton broke it.

"Snow," he said.

"Sir?"

"This ridge on the right. Can we ride along the other side of it, out of sight of the valley?"

Slocum nodded.

"And if I want to," Horton went on, "can I climb it, say, just about where the *rancheria* would be? Maybe a little upstream?"

"Yes, sir."

Slocum could see Horton's plan forming: a cavalry charge, Horton's favorite maneuver. Cross the river a little above the *rancheria,* and then charge right through it. Knock them out with the sheer physical power of the horses bursting right through the encampment. Knock them sprawling, with no time to seize weapons or find a good defense position. Get them worried about the women and children, take the mental high ground from the very start.

Horton grunted with satisfaction. "Good," he said, with

a broad smile. "I will take two companies," he went on crisply. "A and B. I will take them back of the eastern ridge, climb it, go down the other side, cross the river, and charge the *rancheria* from the north.

"Cummings, you will cross the river here." Horton bent down, took the stick Slocum had been using for a pointer, and sketched a line on the dirt map. "Then you will charge the *rancheria* from the south. In preparation, you and I will come into position below the top of the ridge before sunrise. We'll move just before dawn, coming down the ridge to the river as fast as we can. You will cross the river the same way. When we are across we'll charge. If we are seen coming down, we will charge the rest of the way at a gallop. The signal to move will be the rim of the sun coming up over the eastern ridge. Any questions?"

"Yes," Cummings said.

Horton gave him an irritated look. "Well?" he asked.

"How fast does the river flow? Is there quicksand along either shore? Suppose the ground is broken along the valley where you want to make your charge? Suppose—"

"Suppose I am killed by lightning tonight? Suppose my horse stumbles tonight and I break my neck? Suppose, suppose, suppose! There must be an end to supposing or we shall be paralyzed by it. I have come a long way for this fight, and we will charge tomorrow morning."

Several of the officers' faces flushed with excited approval. Cummings waited patiently until they had quieted down.

"Colonel, I do not counsel paralysis. I counsel more scouting."

"There has been plenty of scouting. Time enough tomorrow just before the attack. We can pick out all we need to know with field glasses from the top of the ridge. We'll be plenty close enough then."

"Suppose—" Cummings began.

Horton said, brusquely and rudely, " 'Suppose' again, eh, Cummings? We shall move immediately."

He stood up.

Everyone else stood too. Cummings remained seated.

Slocum shook his head slightly. Cummings had a lot to lose, and Slocum was sure that the captain was pushing his luck.

"One more question, sir."

"What is it, for Christ's sake?"

"Your plan, sir," Cummings said calmly, "calls for the command to be broken into two parts for the attack. Now—"

Horton interrupted with contempt. "I take it," he said, sneering, "that you are going to inform me that a man should never break up his command, because by so doing he weakens it?"

"No," Cummings said calmly. "Your plan depends upon both parts of the command coordinating their movements over insufficiently scouted terrain. How can you be sure—begging your pardon, sir—that they will meet at the same time at the ends of their charges? If one group is delayed by bad ground, the Apaches can deal with that one at their leisure, and then turn to the other and do the same. Now, sir," he went on, "if the ground is not too well known, or if the river is too deep or too fast, or if there should be trouble at the river's edge because of quicksand, how can there be a successful charge? So I suggest we wait for one day for a careful reconn—"

"I see no point in repeating myself," Horton interrupted. He stood up. "Good afternoon, gentlemen."

Lieutenant Palmer snickered. Cummings stood with his hands in his pockets staring up at the dirt map. He took out a cigar and lit it. Then he put his hat on his head squarely and stubbornly. An angry vein pulsed in his cheek, but he shrugged and walked out.

Slocum watched him go. The whole plan gave off a bad smell. He would have ridden away that night, except that he liked Cummings. He decided to stick around for a while.

10

As soon as the sun's rim slid over the eastern horizon Cummings stood up. "Let's go," he said quietly.

They walked up the hill, leading the horses by their reins. The men were very quiet. Several of them owned packs of greasy playing cards. They took them out of their saddlebags and cached them behind rocks. They were superstitious and felt it would be bad luck to die with cards on them.

Cummings did not permit any talking. Slocum brought up the rear and cut short anyone's attempt to speak. The only sounds were the soft creaking of leather gear and the horses' hooves striking against rock. Occasionally a horse snorted or there came the faint jingle of the brass and iron of the harness. These sounds would not carry far. As soon as the command would come within a few miles of their target Cummings intended to muffle the horses' hooves with saddle blankets he'd had the men cut up, and to hell with whatever Horton might think of it.

When they reached the top of the ridge the sun had just cleared the horizon. Slocum could feel it warming the back of his neck. He was grateful for that. The nights could get very chilly at this altitude. The morning was not yet five minutes old, but it was clear that it was going to be a very hot day.

Slocum looked to his right. Along the ridge the men of Horton's B and C companies were just coming over the crest. The two halves of the command started down the hill at the same time. The ground was broken up with gullies and ravines. It was the kind of terrain a more careful and lengthy reconnaissance would have revealed. Slocum didn't like the feel of any of this. He looked at the *rancheria* across the river. A few placid spirals of smoke curled upwards from the jacales. No one was moving down in the cluster of brush huts. Slocum did not like the smell of this at all. Apaches did not sleep late. There was always movement around a *rancheria* at this time: girls going for water with their clay-lined woven baskets, women sitting cross-legged preparing breakfast, little kids running around and screaming and shooting their toy bows and arrows.

He trotted quickly up to Cummings. The older man looked at him. "No good," said Slocum. He jerked his head at the *rancheria*.

"I know goddamn well it's no good," Cummings muttered. He did not want the men to hear him and get panicky.

"So let's sit this one out," Slocum said.

"I'm in the army, Snow," Cummings said. "Whither he goest, I go—god damn the stupid bastard."

Slocum sighed. "Then I'll come along for the ride," he said.

Cummings looked at him with a smile. He shook his head, as if relating a private joke to himself.

"No one's moving down there," Cummings said. "I don't like it."

The river came bouncing down from the mountains, green and cold, like an emerald made out of liquid. Sand cranes stood on sandbars in the river, staring up at the troopers.

It took them ten minutes to ride down to the sandy

beach. The rugged, broken slopes scattered them and slowed them down. They moved in absolute silence, broken only by the thin, brittle jingling of the metal accoutrements of their horses' harnesses. When they reached the river bank, Cummings whispered a command that all carbines be taken out of their saddle scabbards and held high during the crossing. Seasoned troops needed no such reminder, but over half his men had had no combat experience. On this side the bottom of the river seemed solid. He ordered one trooper to snap off dried tree branches and ride ahead, planting them wherever the bottom looked good. Then Cummings kicked his horse into the river. The horse didn't like the cold water and went reluctantly. The water rose to the stirrups, then to the captain's boot tops. He cursed under his breath as his boots suddenly filled with cold water. There had to be snow higher up somewhere, he thought. He was old enough to get a really bad cold out of this. Then the horse began to swim. The current wasn't strong. Cummings figured it would probably sweep them a hundred feet or so downstream. Half a mile ahead, if all went well, Horton's command should be walking into the river about now.

When almost all of the horses were swimming, and just as the corporal with the branches was about to climb up the other shore, the low line of bushes in front of him exploded with carbine fire.

The corporal fell back. He lay dead across the one remaining branch in the shallow water as his riderless horse galloped frantically along the shore. A gray blur moved toward the horse and an arrow buried itself in its withers up to the feathers. The horse pitched and bucked wildly, fell, then thrashed erect, neighing with shrill, penetrating screams in its agony.

The crashing roar of a carbine volley came from Horton's direction. Slocum knew that if they retreated into the river they would be helpless. They would be picked off one by one. The only thing to do was to charge the bushes. Twenty-two men had been hit. A few had slid off their mounts into the current, and the riderless horses milled about frantically in the river, blocking and frightening the other horses.

Cummings had posted Palmer on the far bank to prevent straggling and to keep the men moving. Cummings turned in his saddle and yelled, cupping his hands to his mouth to carry over the firing, the screams of the horses, and the hoarse shouting of the men. "Palmer!" he yelled. "Cover us!" Close to ninety men had not yet put their horses into the river.

Palmer yelled, "Dismount! Fire from prone positions!" A steady, rattling roar came from the bushes. As Slocum dug his spurs into the flanks of his horse, he wondered briefly how it was that the Apaches had known of their approach.

The bullets made the high, screeching sound they made in high altitudes. More men were splashing in the river and dying. A few made it to shore and were cut down immediately. Two more ragged volleys crashed, then Cummings and Slocum hit the far bank. With troopers behind him they spurred up the low, brush-filled slope. Slocum sabered an Apache who rose up behind a dwarf willow and thrust his carbine into Cumming's side without bothering to take aim.

The work was too close for carbines. The men rammed their carbines back into their saddle scabbards and used their Colts. Many of the newer men threw away their carbines in their excitement. In some cases the weapons were flung wildly at the Apaches, who were falling back in good order toward their *rancheria* across the grassy plain.

As soon as Cummings's men had climbed the low bank, Palmer stopped firing. A moment later he was in the river with his men. When he reined in alongside Cummings the

captain yelled, "Column of fours!" Out of the corner of
his eye Cummings noticed that Palmer had a glaring,
frantic look on his face. The young man had behaved
creditably so far, but it was possible that the lieutenant
might turn out to be one of those officers who became
unmanageable in battle—something like a gun-shy hunting
dog.

Cummings looked for the bugler to sound the charge.
Someone yelled that he was dead. Cummings stood up in
his stirrups and yelled, "Fifth Regiment! Trot!" Ten seconds later, when the horses had built up enough momentum,
he called, "Gallop!" Five seconds later he yelled,
"Charge!"

There were no obstacles in front to break the level,
grassy plain. As they thundered on, the men yelling with
excitement and the rage springing from seeing their friends
die in the river, Slocum saw the collection of *jacales*
several hundred yards ahead. To his left, also several
hundred yards away, was the eastern ridge.

There was no one visible in the *rancheria*. No children
or women were running around, the way they would if this
had been a successful surprise attack.

A volley crashed in front. How could they fire so close in
front of us? Cummings thought calmly. From the corner of
his eye he watched Snow riding. Unlike the other officers,
he was lying flat on the withers of his horse. Cummings
smiled in spite of the excitement, the crashing of the
carbines, and the squealing of the horses. There was something about Snow that appealed to him—the man's casual
acceptance of any situation, his amused grin whenever
Horton was more pompous than usual, and his complete
lack of sucking up to the colonel. When this was all over,
Cummings decided, he wanted to get Snow's whole story
out of him.

Another volley. More horses went down, kicking and
squealing. Lieutenant Gibbons, twenty five years old, a

shy, quiet lad from Massachusetts, said quietly, "My God—" and slid from his horse. The horse following his stepped on Gibbons. From the lack of response, Cummings knew that Gibbons was dead. A quick rage against Horton welled up in him. Then Cummings saw that the valley floor was crossed with narrow, shallow ravines, and that the firing came from the ravines, which were too wide to be jumped by a horse moving at a gallop. It was the Little Bighorn all over again.

Cummings threw up his hand. He shouted, "Halt! Dismount!"

When they had dismounted, every fourth man, acting as horse holder, clutched the reins of his own and three other horses. Cummings ran forward to the ravine edge, firing his Colt as he ran. Beside him Slocum trotted, firing slowly and carefully, making each slug count. An Apache suddenly popped up unexpectedly from the heavy cover of tall grass and swung the barrel of his carbine toward Cummings. Before he could pull the trigger Slocum put a bullet in the Indian's chest. The Apache let out a short, strangled yell and fell backward.

Cummings thought, *I owe him one.*

Behind them several riderless horses galloped aimlessly. Firing began at their right and left flanks. The right flank was the river. The Apaches had excellent cover in the thick stand of greenery along the shore. On the left flank the firing came from the hill, where they were hidden in the shallow caves scattered everywhere. Since they were shooting downhill, they overshot. But the splashes their bullets made in the water told them that. Only a few seconds would be necessary to correct their aim.

To charge them would be suicide. Cummings could see one black head, then another circling to their rear. In a few minutes they would be surrounded.

He would have to disobey orders.

"Palmer!" he shouted.

Palmer was loading his Colt. He paid no attention. The air was filled with the neighing of wounded horses, the curses and moans of the wounded men, the shrill exhortations of the Apaches from their superbly concealed crevices, the crash and boom of carbines and an occasional Springfield. The stench of gunpowder and smoke drifted across the grass. Slocum found it incredible to believe that less than a minute had passed since they had begun their charge.

"Palmer!" Cummings shouted.

In his haste the young lieutenant kept dropping cartridges. Palmer looked up, his expression dazed, but he made no sign that he had heard. He went on reloading.

Cummings knew that Palmer was scared. That was normal; he was somewhat scared himself. But Palmer was showing his fear beyond the degree acceptable in an officer in the field. Cummings stood up. Slocum rolled to one side and rested on his elbow, watching. Frightened men were dangerous because they were unpredictable.

Two of Palmer's men got up and started to run for their horses. Slocum permitted himself a small, ironic smile. That was an inevitable result of the fear displayed by an officer who was clearly losing command. Slocum did not move. He knew Cummings would handle the situation well enough.

Sure enough, Cummings belabored their rumps with the flat of his saber. The men fell to the ground, scared and resentful. Palmer just stared, then continued to reload; it gave his hands something to do. Else, Slocum was sure, the young man would get up and his terror-charged body would just run. It was his way of handling his fear. But officers were not allowed this. The man would have to be checked, and that quickly, before his terror began spreading throughout the company.

The firing was getting heavier. "Lieutenant Palmer! God damn it, Palmer!" Cummings shouted. A bullet sliced across his left sleeve. Palmer looked at Cummings for a couple of seconds. He seemed almost about to cry. His face worked and he swallowed. Cummings simmered down. He continued to stand because he knew that his calmness in the face of very clear danger tended to have a soothing effect on terrified men. For a second Cummings actually felt sorry for Palmer. His uncle might not do anything about his nephew's poor behavior in battle, but word would get around, and Palmer would have to face talk of it during the rest of his army career. That would be punishment enough, Cummings considered.

"Lieutenant," Cummings went on, calmly, "we are retreating."

"Huh?"

"We are retreating," Cummings repeated patiently, as if he were in a classroom with a dull pupil, not in the middle of a savage battle. "We will fall back a quarter of a mile or so. We will cross the river any way we can. We will get on the hill—the hill where we left the pack mules. You will fight the rear-guard action. You will fight it especially hard at the ford on this side of the river until the men are across and safe on that hill. Take your wounded with you. I don't have to tell you why. Is that clear?"

Palmer stared without speaking, his face blank.

"Is that clear, Lieutenant?"

Palmer nodded with a dull, stupefied look. Slocum didn't like the expression.

Cummings yelled at the top of his voice, "Lieutenant! I want your men to double up on their horses if necessary. If your men are already doubled up, tell those afoot to grab a stirrup and run alongside. Don't leave the wounded behind to become prisoners."

Slocum knew that Cummings really meant those commands to be heard by the men. It was obvious that he thought Palmer was sure to screw everything up. By pretending to talk to Palmer he was protecting the fearful

young man. Slocum thought it showed a degree of consid-
eration Palmer would never have extended toward Cummings.

"Bugler! Sound 'mount'!"

Cummings looked at Slocum, then up to the ravine
edges and the caves. Words were not needed. Slocum
picked a squad immediately and ordered them to keep up a
heavy fire at the caves and the Apaches who were poking
their heads along the ravines to cover their retreat.

Cummings ordered the men to move and waited till they
had all moved past him. They were all either white and
terrified or flushed and excited. Seeing Cummings, calm
and unmoved, sit his horse steadied them.

The fire of the rear guard suddenly slackened and became weak and sporadic. Cummings turned in his saddle to
see what the problem was.

Palmer had mounted his horse and was screaming at his
men. "Get going! Get going while you can!" He turned
and made for the rear, screaming incoherently. His face
was red and the veins in his throat were almost bursting.
His eyes were open wide. He had left his men flat on their
stomachs. It was a plain case of fear so powerful that it
had taken over completely, a rare enough event in the
professional officer corps. Slocum had only seen one case
of sheer, frantic cowardice in an officer in all his years in
the War, and the man—a captain—had committed suicide
later that night by placing his Colt muzzle in his
mouth.

All of Palmer's men had stopped firing at the Apaches
by the time Palmer's horse had reached Cummings. The
emboldened Indians were kneeling on the ravine edge,
firing at the panicking soldiers. Some of the men were still
on their knees. Others had caught their horses' reins and
were trying to mount the terrified animals. Still others had
abandoned their carbines in their haste to reach their horses
and safety. The Apaches were climbing over the sides of

the ravines, screaming exultantly. One Apache was lancing a soldier whose dead horse lay across his rider's broken thigh.

Cummings reached for Palmer's reins. The lieutenant swung his Colt toward Cummings. Slocum saw Palmer's knuckles tighten on the trigger. If he fired, there would be no way for Cummings to avoid being shot in the chest. And at that close range the impact of the heavy slug would do two things—it would knock him out of the saddle, and he would be shot either in the heart or in the lungs. There was no way for Cummings to knock the gun upward, or to pull his horse out of the way.

There was only one thing Slocum could do.

He shot Palmer dead center in the middle of his forehead.

Palmer fell to his right. His left ankle was jammed into the stirrup, and his horse dragged him and then stopped and stood patiently, turning its head to look at its dead master.

Cummings wasted no time. He shook his head once, slowly. Then he ordered the men to lie flat and begin firing at the advancing Apaches, who were seizing every bit of grass as cover for their erratic advance. Two volleys were enough to force the Apaches back into the ravine, but they had succeeded in whooping several of the riderless horses into a circle. Then they were driven off. In the next minute, two of the horses were killed by the firing from the caves in the cliff. A quick look back through the grass told Cummings that most of the men had reached the shore by now.

By the time Cummings and Slocum and their men reached the river, only three horses and eleven men were still alive. Each horse carried a wounded man across the saddle. Slocum saw bloody lances going in and out of the dead bodies they'd left behind. He sent the wounded across the river. One had a stomach wound and kept screaming like a rabbit being bitten by a coyote.

Only five men now remained on the Apache side of the

river. None of them had a horse. The Apaches began to slide down the bank, heedless of the firing from across the river. They smelled victory and were getting reckless. They dodged behind the driftwood logs and fallen cottonwood trunks brought down by years of heavy spring floods. There they were safe from the shooting from across the river.

Cummings did not want to run the gauntlet of the river under the Apache carbines. There was only one thing to do, and Slocum pointed it out to him.

"Hide in the swamp!" Slocum yelled. A swamp lay to their right. It was a mass of eight-foot-tall cattails with an occasional gnarled willow scattered throughout the cattails. The lavish insect life there attracted birds, but right now they had all flown away because of the noise of the battle.

The men ran as fast as they could for the swamp, splashing up to their knees in the shallows.

Only three of them made it: Cummings, Slocum, and Private Swanson, who had gotten drunk the night before on a bottle of rotgut he had smuggled all this way. He had boasted that he could whip the entire regiment. Right now Swanson had bitten through his lower lip in his frantic dash through the shallows.

When they had gone inside for a hundred feet they stopped. They stood up to their waists in the cold water, panting and sweating. Swanson started to say, "Jesus, Cap'n—" but Cummings hissed a venomous "Shhhh!" at him and the man subsided.

All the sounds of firing had stopped. The Apaches had stopped firing in their direction. Up on the hill, Horton was also silent.

The only sound was the river flowing by a hundred feet away and the wind blowing through the dry stalks of the cattails. The reeds made a faint, dry, clacking rattle very similar to a rattler's warning. The three men stood under the fat brown cylinders of the cattails. It was so still that they could hear the soggy *thump* the cattails made as the wind knocked them together.

"Cap'n," Swanson began again, but he subsided once more at Cummings's angry "Shhhh!"

Slocum tugged Swanson's sleeve and nudged Cummings. He pointed at the nearby willows. They would be on dry land. As Slocum led the way they waded toward the willows as slowly and quietly as possible. Their carbines were held at the ready. The water shallowed. Slocum held up his hand. They stopped. Cummings recognized an expert at work. He yielded leadership easily to a man like Snow. He did not permit any false pride to blind him to common-sense actions. Slocum understood this without any words passing between them.

Cummings waited patiently. Swanson swallowed, nervous. Once more Slocum heard the noise which had made him stop. It was the sound of two of the reeds clacking together. He did not know whether it was made by the wind or the nearly silent passage of an Apache crawling toward them. He pointed the muzzle of his carbine toward the reeds. Cummings nodded and swung the muzzle of his own carbine in short arcs, ready to fire instantly. Swanson's eyes flitted back and forth from one captain to the other.

After three seconds Slocum moved ahead, very slowly. Cummings thought that he had never seen any army officer with such clear evidence of scouting ability; he was sure that Captain Snow—or whatever his name was—had spent many years in interesting occupations, none of which had anything to do with policing the frontier. Quite the opposite, Cummings thought with a broad grin. So quietly did Snow put one foot down before advancing the other that Cummings knew right away that the man must have spent a long time wearing moccasins.

The island toward which Slocum was moving had three cottonwoods on it. Now that they were close to it, Cummings saw it was ten feet by three feet.

Slocum decided that it was clear of Apaches. He turned and waved them on.

So it was only the wind. Cummings let out a long, relieved sigh. Swanson reached out and grabbed a branch that was lying on the ground to pull himself up onto solid ground.

The branch was a snake. Slocum and Swanson saw it at the same time. Slocum acted fast. He clapped one hand over the private's mouth before Swanson let out a terrified yell. When Swanson let out a long sigh of relief, Slocum removed his hand. The three men climbed up onto the island and emptied the water from their boots. The snake was a harmless black snake. It flowed silently into the river and swam away, making arrow-shaped ripples behind it.

The three men sat in a circle. Cummings counted his cartridges. He had five left. Slocum had three. Swanson had abandoned his carbine in his horse's saddle scabbard and had somehow managed to lose all his cartridges in the frantic dash to the swamp. Cummings had his saber. He gave it to Swanson and whispered instructions for its use. "The point, the point, man," he whispered. "Don't swing!"

There was nothing for them to do now but wait for dark. Then they could cross the river and join the men up on the hill. Slocum watched the tops of the cattails. If anyone should try to move through them, the waving brown cylinders would betray his passage. The essential thing now was silence. Sound carried very well across water, and they were surrounded by it.

Slocum saw the tips of three cattails bounce together five feet behind Cummings, but just then a red-winged blackbird flew up from inside the reeds. He thought that the movement of the bird had caused it, and he turned away—something he was to regret for years.

Three seconds later a brown body lunged from the cattails in back of Cummings. Before Slocum could turn around the Apache had driven his eight-foot-long lance clear through Cummings from his left rear. The long, narrow blade emerged from the captain's stomach. Swanson was paralyzed. Slocum grabbed Cummings's saber from Swanson's hand, and in two seconds he had driven the point through the Apache's neck. The man went down, his jugular vein sliced in two. He bubbled his life out in a shrill, triumphant croak. There would be no more danger from him, Slocum saw.

He drove the saber point down into the soggy soil and turned to Cummings.

The captain had slumped to a sitting position. Both of his palms rested on the shaft of the lance. Bright arterial blood welled at the exit hole. Both Slocum and Cummings knew that there was nothing to be done. Swanson knelt beside Cummings and gripped the lance shaft as if to break it off.

Cummings waved him away. "Snow," he said.

Slocum felt bad.

Cummings said, "Swanson, search that Indian for a knife or ammunition."

"Yes, sir."

Cummings had gotten the man out of earshot. "Listen, Snow, or whatever your name is, I know you can get out of here tonight. But since that son of a bitch is going to kill every man in the command, stick around and see that he doesn't. Do me a favor. Take off my wedding ring and give it to my wife. I have a letter from her in my tunic. She's in Omaha. Tell her I wish we could have spent some years together, but that's the way life goes. Tell her I love her. Promise?"

"All right," Slocum said.

"Well, then," Cummings said, satisfied.

When the captain died, Slocum pulled off his gold wedding band. He reached inside the tunic pocket and pulled out a worn, stained letter. The return address read "Mrs. Beulah Cummings. 37 Binney Street, Omaha." He put both objects in his pocket and turned to see Swanson looking at him with a knowing grin.

11

For the rest of the day Slocum and Private Swanson heard an occasional shot from the hill. Bursts of fire came from farther down the river. From mid-afternoon on the firing slackened, though from time to time there was a sudden volley. About four o'clock they heard a loud scream from the edge of the swamp. An hour later revolver firing came from across the river. This slowly trickled away into silence. Then there came a cavalry yell, followed by several more volleys. The firing grew ragged, then became stronger and developed again to volley firing.

It was too confusing for Slocum to figure out. He still hadn't decided whether to oblige Cummings's last wishes. He didn't mind going to Omaha—after all, he had in the past taken quite a few thousand cattle to the stockyards there, mostly rustled, and he liked the town. Mrs. Cummings could wait till his next trip for her ring.

The other request he had granted because the man was dying and it would serve no good purpose to deny Cummings, whom he had begun to like very much, his last wish. But for Slocum to move to join Horton would be suicidal for two reasons. Just to get to where the man was, across country heavily peopled with hostile Apaches, was pure insanity. And then, to face a man whose nephew Slocum had just killed in front of witnesses was asking for

trouble. The most intelligent thing he could do would be to
wait for dark, cut some horse steaks from a dead horse in
the river, and make his way north, traveling at night. He
could make it; he had done things like that before. And to
hell with going up on the hill and taking over from Horton,
which was an idiotic idea anyway. Insane was a better
word for it, even if Colonel Horton was absolutely responsible for all the men who had died today and who would
die tonight.

The sun went down. Slocum sat, not moving. He knew
how to be patient. Swanson was jittery. He kept turning
around, staring into the reeds out of which the Apache had
burst. Slocum felt sorry for the poor kid. He decided to
take him along at least part of the way. He'd point him in
the right direction and let him go. A man like Swanson
would be a millstone around his neck. And one thing was
sure, Slocum was not a gentleman and an officer. He had
not taken any oath to defend the nation. To the contrary,
he had spent four years trying to defeat it. He was under
no obligation to take care of any enlisted man at all. It was
every man for himself, if Horton and the others were all
dead up on that hill.

The sun went down. Twilight deepened. The blue became dark blue, then turned to black. The stars began to
glitter. There was no glow anywhere in the sky. That
meant there would be no moon rising for some time. Give
it half an hour; then he would make his move.

The silence became so intense that Slocum could hear
Swanson's nervous swallows. Finally he touched Swanson's
elbow and tugged at the man's sleeve. Swanson stood up.
Slocum put his palm on top of Swanson's head and pressed
down. Swanson went to his knees.

Slocum led the way. They crawled very slowly. When
they reached the water's edge they placed their legs in the
river slowly. There was not a sound. An occasional shot
sounded from the hill. Once they heard an Apache yell

"How!" as he threw a stone over the packs the mule skinners had set up as a barricade. It was the Apache's way of mocking the white man's greeting.

Suddenly the reeds thinned. Slocum felt the current tugging at him. They could hear drumming coming from the *rancheria*. Thin, piercing screams also came from that direction. The Apaches were busy torturing their prisoners.

The two men went into the stream. The water was ice cold; it was funny Slocum had not noticed it before, but then he had been plunging full tilt for the swamp and had had no attention to spare for what didn't seem absolutely essential at that time.

Slocum gasped as they began swimming, using a breaststroke, making sure their arms did not break the water. They landed on the opposite shore three hundred yards downstream. Very slowly, lest their feet should knock one stone against another, they crawled flat up onto the shore. A match flared fifty feet away.

"There are the troops!" Swanson said jubilantly, and Slocum elbowed him to silence.

The match was put out.

They saw Apache lances against the sky and slid back into the river. The Apaches heard them turn back and called out, "Are you afraid? We are not white troops."

In their hissing, guttural tongue Slocum said, "We were afraid, yes!"

They floated downstream with the current for another hundred yards. There was no sound of pursuit. They edged inshore again at the debouching of a small ravine.

This was where Slocum had intended to say goodbye to Swanson, give him his blessings, and then take off, drifting down the river for a few miles. He had planned to cut off a few steaks from the first dead horse he came across. "Well, Private," he said softly, "here's where we part company."

"*What?*" Swanson said. His mouth gaped open.

"Goodbye." Slocum's voice was hard.

"Cap'n Snow, what *am* I gonna do?" Swanson reached out to grab Slocum's sleeve, and by accident his hand slid into Slocum's. He was like a small child asking to be taken across a dangerous street, and suddenly Slocum knew there was no way he could leave this helpless, inexperienced youngster behind. He could either take him along and be burdened with him all the way to the border, or he could take Swanson and go to join Horton. That might be even more foolish, but suddenly he felt an obligation to the rest of the men in the command, all of whom might yet die under torture, like the ones whose agonized screams they had heard back at the swamp, unless somehow he could change what was sure to happen up there on the hill.

And, what the hell—he had made a promise. And Slocum prided himself on keeping his word.

"I'll tell you what we're going to do, Swanson. We're going to follow this ravine up to the hill, and then we're going to join the rest of the command."

"Well, hallelujah," breathed Swanson. "*Hallelujah!*"

They still had the problem of getting past the Apaches who were clustered in the ravines running up to the crest of the hill where Horton's men lay surrounded.

Slocum took off his hat and tore his uniform blouse into a square. When he had put it over his head and tied his bandanna around it the dark cloth, in the moonless night, could pass for the shoulder-length hair of an Apache.

He was sure he could get away with it. No one would be expecting a white soldier to be coming up in the dark to rejoin his comrades. Sure enough, fifty feet ahead an Apache was squatting in the ravine eating some jerky.

Slocum disposed of him quietly. He dragged the body behind a boulder, and stripped it of its breechclout and knee-high moccasins. He took off his uniform trousers, boots, and underwear, and donned the Apache garb. A lance was resting against the ravine wall. He bundled up his clothes and boots and handed them to Swanson.

"Keep your mouth shut," Slocum whispered. "You're my prisoner, understand?"

"Yes, sir, Cap'n, sir!"

Good, Slocum thought. *Swanson looks scared enough.*

Slocum picked the lance up in his left hand. In his right he held his saber. The lance would complete the illusion he was seeking. Who but an Apache would carry a lance?

Within fifty feet someone called out, "Have you come to join the party?"

"I took this White Eyes!" Slocum laughed triumphantly. He waved his saber aloft, and then deliberately struck Swanson in the buttocks. The sincerely aggrieved yell brought shouts of laughter from the warriors who were sitting or lying all the way up the ravine, waiting for the dawn charge.

"Move, move, you sunnabitch!" Slocum said, using the English word at the end of the sentence in Apache. While the rest of the Apaches grinned in envy—none of them had yet taken a prisoner—Slocum and the private climbed the slope. In a very few minutes they were within twenty-five yards of the command.

Every Apache in the ravine was looking at them. Slocum silently thanked God for the year he had spent with the Chiricahua learning their language.

"I will charge them myself, and use this Melikana shit for a shield," Slocum cried.

No one tried to dissuade him. Indian warfare was as democratic an arrangement as possible, and each warrior accepted the war chief's authority as long as he felt like it. There were no sanctions if a man just didn't feel like fighting in any particular engagement. It was his medicine that told him to do it, and no Indian would ever quarrel with that. So there was silence. If a man felt his medicine would protect him in what others felt might be a suicide charge, that was his business.

He pushed Swanson roughly over the edge of the ravine. Ahead of them were some packs being used as breastworks.

Swanson stumbled and fell flat. Slocum prodded him in the buttocks once more. Swanson's agonized yell, as Slocum had hoped, attracted the command's attention.

Slocum yelled, "Company A and B! Hold your fire! This is Captain Snow coming in with Private Swanson!" Then he added in Apache, for the benefit of the men behind him—none of whom, he hoped, spoke English—"I come, *yahezine!*"

There was a startled silence behind him. Then came a great, admiring laugh. The word meant, literally, *Those who stand facing downhill.* This was a reference to the frequently observed fact that cattle on a slope stand facing downward. The implication that the besieged soldiers at the top of the hill were all facing downhill like cattle was, in Apache, a superb joke.

And any suspicion about what Slocum might have said in English was completely swept away.

Slocum and Swanson ran as fast as they could toward the barricade and slid over the packs. A trooper saw the Apache clothes Slocum was wearing and raised his revolver. Slocum slapped him in the chest with his open palm, saying, "I'm Captain Snow!"

Swanson was flat on the ground, gasping and shuddering for breath. The Apaches suddenly understood that they had been tricked. The slope below erupted with orange flashes.

Slocum grinned. "They just caught on," he said to Swanson.

"What?" the terrified private asked.

Slocum realized that he would miss Cummings in more than one way.

"Where's my boots and clothes?" he asked.

Swanson was still clutching them. He handed them over. "Anyone got a canteen?" Swanson asked plaintively.

"No water," someone said. "We ain't had none all day."

It was Corporal Rigby who spoke. He added, "The colonel wants to see you right away."

Slocum noticed that the word "sir" was missing. He would take this up with the corporal later.

"And he wants Captain Cummings. Real fast, the both of you."

The hell with waiting, Slocum thought.

"I'm not in uniform, Corporal," he said.

Rigby was a big man with massive arms. He had the air of confidence which probably came from winning fist-fights easily, Slocum thought. It was clear that Rigby was simply parroting Horton's opinion of Slocum. Rigby felt sure, no doubt, that any complaint Slocum made to Horton about the colonel's orderly would be summarily dismissed.

"Aw, shit," Rigby said contemptuously. He weighed thirty pounds more than Slocum.

"I want an outward show of respect from you, Corporal, whenever you talk to me," Slocum said.

"Aw, shit," Rigby said once more, and turned on his heel.

Slocum reached out and spun the man by his right elbow till he faced to his right, as if he made a parade ground right face. Slocum's right fist sank deep into Rigby's solar plexus. Rigby let out an agonized *whoosh!* and slumped to his knees, holding his paralyzed stomach with both hands.

"Next time say 'sir'," Slocum said mildly.

He wouldn't have bothered with this performance if he hadn't decided that some type of command would devolve upon him since Cummings's death. Something had to be done to prove that discipline existed, or everyone up on the hill would be having a very hard time. There was no

water, to start with. The next day was going to be a very
hot one and there was no shade anywhere.

Slocum waited three seconds. Sure enough, Rigby started
to unbutton the flap of his Colt. Slocum took a step and
kicked Rigby's wrist. The Colt soared up and fell at
Swanson's feet. He was too scared to move.

"Give it back to him," Slocum told the private.

Swanson would be sure to spread the story around. Half
crouched, Slocum put on his pants and blouse, then pulled
his boots on. His stockings had been abandoned somewhere
down in the ravine. He'd need another pair quickly, or else
he'd develop blisters.

Someone said respectfully, "Sir, the colonel's over down
the hill a ways ."

"Thanks," Slocum said. It was clear to all that Captain
Snow did not take it kindly if the word "sir" was omitted,
but that if it was used, he had good manners.

He found Horton in the darkness. It was Horton; Slocum
could tell by the distance placed between that dark shadow
and everyone else.

"Snow?" The colonel's voice was harsh.

"Yes, sir."

"You murdering son of a bitch!"

12

Strange to say, Slocum had forgotten all about shooting Lieutenant Palmer. Now it all came back to him. Things were going to be worse than he had anticipated. How could he do any kind of remedial work up here on the hill, surrounded by Apaches, without water, and confronted with a colonel who had just made that kind of accusation? Slocum was beginning to regret his decision to keep his promise to the dying Cummings.

It would be wise for him to say nothing until Horton spoke again. Slocum crossed his arms and remained silent.

"We're facing a serious problem up here," Horton said abruptly. "Where's Cummings?"

"Dead," Slocum said laconically.

Horton was silent for three seconds. "How?" he asked.

"Apache lanced him."

"That makes you my senior officer, Snow. I'll deal with you later. First things first."

They had met with such a terrific concentration of fire when they had crossed the river that Horton had decided to turn back immediately. They had ridden into an ambush. Slocum thought of the old saying: *Time spent in reconnaissance is never wasted*.

Once across the river again, they had tried to climb the hill and find a defensive position. But it was so steep that they made very bad time, and too many men were being shot off their horses by the heavy fire from below. Horton halted, dismounted what was left of the command, and had them fight right where they stood.

The Apaches must have known of the attack and how it would come, Horton said now. One of them must have picked up the scouts' tracks and followed them back to camp. Then he had trotted back with the information that the soldiers would be coming. So they had men on the east side of the river; they came out of the ravines which were all over the east side of the hill. All the ravines connected with each other. Two of them joined together above the final position taken by Horton and the remnant of his command. So they were completely surrounded.

"So they have perfect cover and communication, and we have neither?" Slocum asked.

Horton nodded grudgingly. His eyes were filled with hatred. He would have liked to kill Snow right then, but who would assume the necessary functions of the second officer in command?

"How many Apaches are around us?"

"Ever take a stick and stir up an ant heap?" Horton asked. "They came boiling around us so fast and furious I couldn't count them."

"Only way I can figure it out is that there are plenty of *rancherias* in the adjoining valleys," Slocum said thoughtfully. "They must have gotten together after we had done our scout, even in the little time they had."

Horton flushed at the implied criticism, but he chose to disregard it. He would handle that later, after they were out of this mess, Slocum knew.

When the command had arrived, the Apaches had sprinkled a little sugar for the white soldiers by showing them an empty *rancheria* in the grama grass. And, just like flies, Horton had sent his men across the river. He was too greedy for quick results. Another commander would have asked for further reconnaissance, particularly after the Custer fiasco. None of this would look good in the reports, and Slocum did not see how Horton would be able to cover up.

If they got out of this alive.

"How! How! How!"

"Hold your fire!" Horton yelled. That, at least, was a sensible order. In the darkness, perfectly protected by their ravines, the Apaches were trying to draw the soldiers' fire, make them reveal their positions and waste ammunition.

Across the river there were several camp fires. Both men realized that prisoners were being tortured at that very moment.

"Have we got good defensive positions?" Slocum asked.

"Who the hell knows?" Horton asked curtly.

"Mind if I check them out?" Slocum persisted.

Horton shrugged.

Slocum stood up. He made his way at a half crouch to the perimeter. The top of the hill was almost flat. Its inner surface had a small circular depression, almost like a very shallow cup. The remaining mules and horses were corralled there. The men had dug in with their knives and sabers and piled up the dirt to make a crude breastwork wherever there weren't sufficient packs from the pack train. There had been some grass there, but by then the mules and horses had cropped it as smooth as a croquet lawn. At least the moisture in the grass would keep the animals from being too thirsty the next day. The day after that would see problems beginning for them. The men would start showing the effects of thirst by tomorrow afternoon. Slocum wished that he had taken as much water as he could drink when he had been in the swamp down below.

Several men were kneeling around a reclining figure

who whimpered and and spoke in Apache. Slocum walked over and the men fell back. He knelt and ran his hand over the person. He felt a buckskin skirt and the Apache knee-high women's moccasins. He ran his hand up and felt breasts and, higher up, a wrinkled face. It was an old Apache woman. Her hands were tied behind her back.

"What the hell's going on here?" he asked the troopers. There was silence.

The woman cried softly. "My hand," she said in Apache. She had no way of knowing that Slocum spoke her language. He turned her over. Someone had cut off her index finger. Slocum took out his knife and she whimpered in fear, but he cut the rope tying her wrists.

"Colonel ain't gonna like that," someone said.

Slocum took out his handkerchief and bandaged the stump of her finger.

"Who did this?" he asked.

Silence again.

"You!" Slocum grabbed the man who had said the colonel wouldn't like it. With both hands he pulled him close to his own hard face.

"Once more—what's going on?"

The man decided he had better talk. "Comin' up the hill, sir, we came across this old bitch pickin' medicine plants or somethin'. The colonel he says grab 'er. So we did. For tradin'."

Slocum looked at the old woman. Whether Apache women did the torturing at their *rancherias* or not—and Slocum did not have the slightest doubt that they did—he was not going to see this old woman tortured.

"Who cut her finger off?" he asked.

Silence again. Someone said slowly, "None of us did it, Cap'n."

"That's for danged sure!" someone else added.

"If Colonel Horton didn't do it," Slocum said, "just say so."

The silence that followed was a clear enough reply for Slocum.

"All right," Slocum said. He turned to the old woman, who was whimpering in pain. She was about seventy, Slocum judged, but it was hard to be sure. When Indians passed fifty it was difficult to guess their ages; their life was so hard.

"*Iszanale se*," he said. The old woman jerked up her head. He had called her White Painted Woman, the most important female deity of the Chiricahua. She was the mother of Child of the Water, their culture hero. It was a term of the most serious respect.

"Come."

She stood up, her face alert, and he took her elbow.

"You lettin' her go, Cap'n? I gotta tell the colonel—he told me to guard 'er."

"Do your duty, soldier," Slocum said calmly. The man ran at a crouch toward Horton while Slocum took the old woman to the barricades. He called out into the darkness, in Apache, "We are sending you back one of your old women. Don't shoot."

She crawled over the barricade and went downhill swiftly on her hands and knees, calling out to her people. They apparently recognized her voice and held their fire. *Thank God,* Slocum thought.

"Colonel wants to see you, Cap'n," someone said. "He says *right now*."

The wounded were beginning to cry out for water. Horton was sitting cross-legged on the ground. His shoulders were covered by a saddle blanket. By now a sickle moon had risen. For the first time since Slocum had met Horton he saw gray stubble on the man's face. It came as a shock. Slocum had never thought of Horton as being any particular age.

Horton threw off the blanket as soon as he saw Slocum.

He said, in a cold rage, "Your orders were to charge the *rancheria*. You did not. Therefore I was forced to withdraw. The failure of the operation must be laid at your feet."

Slocum had to admire the man's ability to behave as if he were a professor in a classroom. "Sir—" he began.

"Let me finish, Snow! You ordered that filthy old squaw to be released. Who the hell are you to go against my special orders?"

"Someone had cut off her finger. I don't think any purpose could be served by—"

"You killed my nephew, you murdering son of a bitch!"

"He tried to shoot Captain Cummings."

"*What?* Are you insane?"

"No, sir. The lieutenant wasn't able to control himself in battle, and in his rush to get away he was so frantic that he pulled his gun on Cummings. I had no choice but to shoot him."

"You're an incompetent maniac!" the colonel declared.

"Am I relieved from duty?"

"No. I've lost too many officers! And there's one more reason why I'm not having you shot immediately. I want this entire affair of your fantastic assumption of authority from me to be thrashed out in a court-martial when we get back to Fort Grant. Is that clear?"

"Yes, sir."

All right. Slocum thought he could go along with that nonsense for a while. It was obvious that Horton would try to convince whatever board would hear the evidence that there was only one reason why his expedition had become a fiasco—and that reason was Captain Snow's incredible behavior. It would be Snow who would take Horton off the hook. Shooting a brother officer, freeing an Apache prisoner, refusing to obey Horton's explicit tactical orders—all these would be important to Horton at a show trial. No wonder Horton didn't want to shoot him on the spot.

"When we get back I'll show you there's a God in Israel!"

Not a sound came from the men. Horton was yelling so loud that his voice carried everywhere.

"Sir. Since you are leaving me in command up here, I suggest that you not speak to me this way in front of the men. You will only weaken discipline, and we will have need of discipline before this work is done." Slocum stood with his right hand on the butt of his Colt. Rigby, the colonel's orderly, stood behind Horton and a few inches to his right. If Rigby were to pull his Colt, he would sear the colonel's face with its muzzle blast. The thought must have occurred to Rigby, and he moved a foot more to his right. It was a tense situation, but Slocum could see humor in it. Here he was facing a standoff on this hill in Mexico with an army colonel, as if they were two gamblers in a cowtown saloon.

"Don't tell me—" Horton began. Then he suddenly subsided. He had recognized the truth in Slocum's remark. He had regained control to a remarkable degree. He was once more the dashing cavalry officer. He turned to Rigby and motioned downward with the flat of his opened hand. Slocum was amused to see Rigby remove his hand from his gun butt, almost as if he were a growling watchdog which had been told to relax by its master.

Horton beckoned Slocum closer. When Slocum bent down Horton said softly, "Snow, did you kill that boy because you and he had words once?"

"No, sir."

"And did you use that trumped-up story of cowardice to throw mud on the poor boy's reputation? Eh?"

Slocum simply shook his head. He was awed by Horton's busily working mind.

Horton clenched his teeth. "Speak up, Snow!" He pulled his blanket tighter around himself.

"No, sir."

Slocum's calm tone inflamed Horton. "How the hell do you know that the boy wasn't intending to shoot one of the goddamned Apaches? Eh? And then you seized upon that quarrel between Cummings and the lad to kill him."

"No, sir, I did not." Slocum spoke calmly once more and waited. This son of a bitch was a little too crazy for him. Slocum decided he had better put an end to it and get out, and to hell with his promise to Cummings.

Horton sat inside his blanket. He looked like a Sioux himself, except for his gray stubble. "Snow—" he began. But just then a flight of fire arrows hissed through the air. One sank three inches into a mule. The animal's screams cut short their discussion.

Down the hill voices were raised. "*Al frente,* Belikan! *Vamos hablar poquito! Estamos amigos!* Up in front, Americans! Let's talk a bit! We're friends!"

They called all night long. In between there were more arrows and an occasional shot. It was obvious that the Apaches wanted to keep them awake, to weaken the soldiers. Not a bad strategy, Slocum thought; the Apaches could take turns, so that every one of them could get plenty of sleep and food. Weakened soldiers did not fight well or intelligently.

Horton had reluctantly dismissed him. The few officers had to take over the duties of the dead sergeants as well as those of the dead officers. Slocum crawled along the perimeter and checked on the sentries' vigilance. Satisfied, he found a blanket, rolled up, and fell asleep immediately. He was exhausted. Tomorrow was another day.

He woke up once. His mouth was dry and he would have given anything to have drunk his fill of water down in the swamp before he came up the hill. Tomorrow was another day, yes—and it looked like it was going to be a very hard one. The lack of water for the second day up there on an exposed position would provide serious problems.

And to solve problems a man needed energy. Slocum willed himself to sleep once more.

13

When Slocum awoke, the sun was well up. Across the river countless Apaches were milling about in the *rancheria*. Some of the troopers were putting pebbles in their mouths to stave off the effects of thirst. Others were chewing the few blades of grass they could find after the mules and the horses had finished their grazing. Each blade might yield a tiny bit of moisture.

In the middle of their dry breakfast of hardtack and jerky, the Apache attack came.

The Indians had crawled along the bottom of a ravine till they came close to the hilltop. The sentries were completely unaware of their approach until they suddenly burst from the ravine as quickly as their own mountain quail. One second they were completely invisible, the next second the air seemed to be full of Apaches in war paint, black and yellow slashes across their faces, black eyes searing with hatred. They screamed and whooped, trying to stampede the horses, but the mounts were too solidly picketed—Slocum had seen to that during the night—and aside from plunging, rearing, and snorting, nothing happened.

Through volley after volley the Apaches tried to scramble up the slope. Slocum walked back and forth, talking softly and calmly. "Wait till I give the order to fire," he

said. "Fire low. Don't aim any higher than their bellies."
Slocum knew the tendency to overshoot when firing
downhill. Aiming low would bring the bullet impact up to
chest level.

Another charge came up the hill with shouts of "American
pigs!"

The carbines became overheated and began to jam. The
extractors had cut through the rims of the shells as though
they were made from putty. They left the unexploded
cartridges wedged solidly in the firing chambers.

"Gouge 'em out with your knives!" Slocum ordered.

"Lost m' knife," several of the men shouted back.
Slocum pulled all the men who still had knives out of the
line and gave them the job of extracting the jammed
cartridges. The cartridge casings were made of copper that
was too soft. They were carried in leather loops on their
belts. The chemical reaction of the copper and the leather
caused verdigris to form, and that made the cartridges
much harder to extract. It was something Slocum would
not have permitted had he been in the War Department in
Washington. The army moved ponderously. Whenever it
faced a problem its response was too slow, and people
died on the frontier until the error was eliminated. Too
many manufacturers put pressure upon their friends in the
Quartermaster Corps not to move hastily. Tooling new
machines would be too expensive; soft copper was cheaper
than the harder kind—it was a comedy of delay. But here
on this hilltop in Mexico it could easily turn into tragedy.
Slocum could not have remained in such an army and
escaped from the charge of mutiny or insubordination. He
knew he had survived in the Confederate Army during the
War because he operated in small units behind the lines
and supplied himself with the best material that he could
capture, commandeer, or just plain steal. Slocum had never
used cartridges encased in soft copper. He always bought
better cartridges and, so far, they'd helped him survive.

Several Apaches burst from the ravine far to the right and began running along the hill as if they were following contour lines. They leaped and shouted and, turning their buttocks toward the hilltop, they slapped themselves.

"Jesus," breathed one of the soldiers, a man named O'Hara. "What the devil are they up to?"

"Showing us how brave they are," Slocum said. "Hold your fire till they get close!"

The roar of the carbines traveled down the barricade from the right. The roar reminded Slocum of the sweep of a summer thunderstorm over hard ground, only quite a bit louder.

"Ah," said O'Hara suddenly, in an annoyed, almost calm voice. A bullet had carried away the bridge of his nose as well as his right eye. He turned and squatted down beside Slocum, who thought that the man must be in shock. But O'Hara hung his head calmly and dug out the coagulating blood from his empty eye socket. After he had gotten some out he held his hand out to Slocum.

"Cap'n," he said, "look 'n' see if that ain't my brains."

"No, it isn't," Slocum said, half disgusted, half amused. "You damn fool—you wouldn't be talking any more if that was your brains. Lie down and don't move."

"If you say so, Cap'n," O'Hara said, and followed orders.

It was quiet for a while. The Apaches had sunk back into their network of ravines, leaving four dead behind them. That was a high percentage of casualties for Apaches, who preferred to employ guerrilla tactics and take no losses; four dead for the Apaches was far more serious to them than ten times that number for the cavalry. Slocum was sure that their impetuous attacks and willingness to take such losses was due to their desire to force Horton to pull out rather than lose more men. After all, this place had been the secret Apache stronghold and refuge since the

Spaniards had first invaded this land, over which the Apaches had once exercised total domination.

The troopers' thirst grew worse. This was the second day up on the hill for the men. In the excitement of the struggle to get up there, no one—not even Horton—had thought they'd be there for long, so no orders had been given to ration the water in their canteens. Now the canteens were empty. It was Horton's fault, as commander, and the realization of it did not improve the colonel's temper.

Horton stood up and walked over to O'Hara. The wounded man had wrapped his neckerchief around the missing eye so that he resembled a pirate. "Where'd they get you, son?" Horton asked.

O'Hara pointed silently.

"Give 'em 'Hail Columbia', boys," the colonel said loudly. "They've spoiled O'Hara's beauty." A laugh went up, just as Horton had calculated it would. Then Slocum watched as Horton made a tour of the hilltop, patting a man here, laughing there. What amused Slocum was the deliberate and conniving way Horton did it, as if he planned to write the incident in his memoirs, with the chapter heading of "Besieged Colonel Raises Men's Spirits."

Then Slocum noticed the drawn, pinched look on Horton's gray-stubbled face. For a strong command like his to be lured into such a trap would not look good when General Dodge sat down to read it in Omaha. No subtle blandishments or evasions could conceal the facts. Horton had blundered right into a massive ambush. It might very well ruin his subsequent army career, not to mention his political aspirations. He had placed himself in a situation where he would very likely, thought Slocum, lose all sense of proportion.

The only way Horton could dig himself out of this mess with any credit would be to kill great numbers of Apaches. That might be sold to Washington as the justification for his bold entry into the heart of Apache country. And Slocum felt sure that would be the purpose of this day on the hill.

Slocum turned to look down the hill just as a bullet struck the mound of dirt someone had hurriedly thrown up with a knife. The impact threw so much dirt into Slocum's eyes that he could not see for several minutes. He lay there, blinking and tearing. As he pulled down his upper eyelids over the lower ones a bullet fired from a Springfield rifle a quarter of a mile away from the adjoining hill crest struck his right boot and tore the heel off. Still blinded, Slocum crawled away and waited for his sight to return.

A sudden thump of bowstrings sounded from a ravine. Slocum instinctively rolled himself into a ball in order to make a smaller target. The flight of arrows sailed overhead. One of them struck Swanson's yellow bronco in the withers. The horse squealed and reared. The sudden rear pulled out its picket pin. It raced across the hill, bucking and pitching, in a vain attempt to shake the arrow loose. Another series of bucks and the horse had cleared the barricade. It raced at an angle down the ridge, dragging the long picket rope behind it. As soon as it reached the first clump of chaparral the picket pin tangled itself in the brush. The horse halted, trembling and squealing in pain. Swanson half rose. The yellow bronco was his one passion.

An Apache emerged from the ravine close to the clump of chaparral. He grabbed the picket pin and started to untwist the rope from the chaparral. It was safe enough, since he kept the horse between himself and the hilltop. No one fired; the risk of hitting Swanson's beloved mount was too great.

From the corner of his tearing eyes Slocum saw a flash of blue. Swanson was tumbling over the barricade. He landed on his knees and ripped his trousers.

"Swanson!" Slocum yelled. "Get back!"

The man ignored him. Sobbing in rage and terror, Swanson picked himself up and started to run downhill toward his horse.

"Get back, *get back,* you damn fool!" Slocum yelled.

The man kept running. "All right, trooper," Slocum yelled, wiping his eyes, "you'll catch hell when you come back! Fire and cover him!" he ordered the men.

Swanson had to run one hundred fifty feet before he could reach his horse. The Apache heard the roar from the top of the hill. He jerked his head around and saw the trooper running toward him. The Apache pulled a knife and waited. He realized he could not untwist the line in time. He could have cut the line in the beginning, but he had wanted the picket pin for himself.

Swanson had his revolver out when he came to the horse, but the Indian dodged expertly, always keeping the horse between them, waiting for a chance to use his knife without getting shot. For a brief moment the two men danced in a game of hide-and-seek.

The Apache was too agile for Swanson, who was afraid of firing so close to his beloved horse. Swanson suddenly realized that he also had a knife in his pocket. With his left hand he extracted his jackknife and opened the blade with his teeth, chipping one of his incisors as he did so. Cutting the horse free, he slid easily onto its bare back and rode toward the troopers at a gallop, lying flat on its back. He made it to the barricade without getting shot. Then, directly in front of Slocum, the horse suddenly reared and neighed as two bullets struck its buttocks. Swanson slid off, ran his hands over the holes from which blood was pouring, and remounted. He cantered a few steps. A ragged volley came from the Apaches. The horse stumbled and fell with a broken shoulder. Swanson went rolling. He stood up and a bullet caught him in the head and he went down. The horse kept screaming in agony until Slocum put a bullet through its head.

Hours later. The sun was directly overhead. Across the river in the *rancheria* they could see objects scattered here and there. They were white and looked like bones at this distance, but everyone knew what they were—the naked bodies of the dead, tortured prisoners.

Slocum had the men spread their blankets over vertical sticks and whatever else could provide support. Any shade would make the heat draw out less water from their already parched bodies. Horton sat staring into space and made no effort to take control. He was satisfied to let Slocum do what he wished. Rigby took up his station close to his colonel with a worried look. The hills around them shimmered and shook in the heat haze.

Slocum thought about Swanson. He was the one the squad had sent one night to draw saber ammunition, and the next night they sent him to make a social call upon Colonel Horton. "Sure," they told him, "the colonel's lonely out here, and he sure appreciates a heart-to-heart talk with the men. We rotate talkin' to him, you see, and tonight it's your turn. You just walk right into his tent; he likes bein' informal. You'll see."

And Swanson had gone.

Slocum wished Cummings were here. He'd say something like, "I wouldn't've gone across that stretch of ground for all the horses in the United States—and that nervous buck private went for one yellow bronco!"

The wounded were crying for water now. *Down below, maybe three hundred yards*, Slocum thought, *is a cold green river. It's there for the taking—all the water a thirsty man could want.*

"Will you look at that red son of a bitch?" shouted Corporal Moran. "Will you be lookin' at him now?"

Slocum turned. A bare arm waved derisively from the edge of a ravine. A voice yelped, "How, how, how!" After their attention had been secured, the hand withdrew and emerged again holding a small clay pot. The pot tilted and water spilled out. "Cold, cold, *cold!*" the voice chanted, and laughed. Then the empty pot was withdrawn. Several times water was flung up into the air. Voices filled the entire ravine as they took up the call of "Cold, cold, cold!"

A harsh voice suddenly called, "Come, soldiers! We no kill. Come get water. We send you back all right, no shoot. Yes, Yes, Yes!"

The pot went aloft again. It poised, and very slowly the bearer let the water trickle out. Slocum looked right and left. Most of the men were licking their lips.

A shot rang out and the pot exploded. In the shattered debris that sprayed over the ravine was the Apache's amputated forefinger. A loud yell of surprise and dismay came from the ravine.

All along the barricade a roar of laughter swelled. Rigby put down his carbine. The men were grinning and pointing at him with admiration.

"Good shootin', Rigby," someone said.

"Don't get so riled up," Rigby said, with sullen ferocity. "Plenty officers got killed that way in the War. Easy as pie to shoot one in the back in one of them skirmishes." He added with intensity, "But no officer went 'n' shot another officer like Cap'n Snow did. The son of a bitch shot the lieutenant deliberate. He pulled his gun an' shot him right smack dab in the middle of his forehead. Someone who saw it told me, an' someone else saw it an' told me. I got two witnesses who seen it. That's murder. I don't see why the colonel don't jus' stand 'im up 'gainst the barricade 'n' shoot 'im right now. Cap'n Snow was a buddy of Cummings, and that fat son of a bitch never got along with the colonel—always givin' 'im lip. So Snow shot the lieutenant, figurin' no one would know, they bein' in a skirmish 'n' all down there. Jus' wait till we get back to Fort Grant. That'll be the end of Cap'n Snow. Jus' you wait!''

''I dunno,'' the other man said. ''Cap'n Snow looks like he knows what he's doin'. I says if he shot Palmer, then that shavetail deserved it. I say—''

''Don't crowd me,'' Rigby said with a chill hatred that barred any further discussion. ''Or I'll use your skull bone to keep my cufflinks in.''

The thud of bowstrings came from a ravine. A trooper suddenly stood erect with a bewildered expression, lifted a hand to his ear, then crumpled to his knees, shaking his head as if he were a horse shaking off an annoying fly. An arrowhead had penetrated the bone behind his ear. The arrowhead had gone in its full length. Slocum could see the tail of the arrowhead, which was fastened to the reed shaft with a little deer sinew.

''Doc!'' the cry went up. The doctor was crouching in a makeshift tent operating on a shattered shoulder, heedless of the cries of pain and the calls for water.

''Is the man conscious?'' the doctor asked. When he was answered yes, he asked, ''What's the arrow made of? Hoop iron or steel?''

''Hoop iron.''

''Lay him down and leave the arrow alone.''

''How 'bout breakin' it off, doc?''

''A fine way to kill him if it's near the brainpan. Might fracture the skull if you wiggle the shaft any.''

When the man was brought in the doctor had finished bandaging his patient. Now he turned to examine the new man.

''Get me a pair of pliers,'' he ordered.

He hefted the pliers and looked at Slocum. ''I think you had better do this, Snow,'' he said. ''I need someone strong. Just pull straight out. Not sideways—not a *fraction* of an inch. A slow, steady pull. Can you do it?''

''If a couple of men hold him,'' Slocum replied.

Two men held the wounded man. Slocum pulled the arrowhead out, but he lifted all three men, as the arrowhead was quite crooked.

The doctor began bandaging the man. He shook his head at the cries of the wounded for water. "I don't know what to do," he said helplessly.

Slocum heard the peculiar thud which announced the breaking of a bone by a bullet. A trooper a few feet away put his hand to his head and said in amazement, "I'm hit." He fell. He could not see or hear and his feet kept kicking feebly till he was removed to the makeshift hospital.

"Keep low!" snapped Slocum. "Any volunteers to get that sniper?"

Someone whispered, "Two hundred feet to the first ravine. Then a series of ravines, all jammed full of 'paches like peas in a pod, and then a small climb of two hundred more feet directly up the hill where the sniper sits waitin'. This here mother's boy is stayin' right here."

Slocum silently agreed, but still he said, "Come on, troopers—who will skip that fellow out?"

Silence.

"Can't say I blame you fellows," Slocum said.

"No chance, no chance, eh?" demanded Horton. He sat up, his back rigid. "It has come to my attention," he began, as if he were sitting in the officers' mess at Fort Grant, "that some of my official actions have been criticized. While I am willing to take recommendations from any junior second lieutenant, it will have to come through proper channels." He glared at Slocum, who began to realize that quite possibly Horton's mind had snapped.

"Sir—" Slocum began. But Horton cut him off abruptly. "I am not here to be catechized by you, Captain! You have bitten off more than you can chew. And the chewing is bound to take considerable time." He turned to the men. "If there are no volunteers, *all* of you will suffer, I can promise you that!"

He turned and looked across the river to the *rancheria*. All that could be seen was dust and horses. Then the dust cleared.

"Look!" he shouted. "Look down there! They've made spread eagles of the men!" He turned abruptly and walked away.

Slocum immediately sensed that the men were badly shaken by this display of despair on the part of their commander.

"You, you, you!" he called out crisply. "I want all the dead horses dragged to make a circle around the hospital. Then tie the reins of the live mounts to their legs. It'll hold better than the picket pins." He added, "You there! Why didn't you reload?"

"I didn't think there was any use. I thought there was no danger." Under Slocum's stare the man added, "Cap'n, sir." The trooper stared sullenly at the ground.

"You *what?*"

"The 'paches ain't gonna attack in broad daylight, sir."

"No danger—no danger. I have seen a great many 'no danger' men in the mountains, trooper. Most of them were dead, like those across the valley. Listen to me carefully. You are *always* in danger in Indian country. *Reload!*"

The man disliked him, Slocum saw. But now he had them all busy, dragging horses, pulling out picket pins, making the living horses' reins fast to the legs of the dead ones. The chastised private was reloading. The spurt of action kept their minds off what was happening to their friends over in the *rancheria*. It was something Horton should have attended to. Slocum knew it was a good idea, in circumstances where great tension existed, to behave like a firework—always going bang at someone. None of the men knew who would be getting it next, and it kept their bodies and minds busy.

But they'd have to get some water tonight. They couldn't last another day.

A man sighed and said, almost apologetically, "There's plenty of good water down there, Cap'n. I'm goin' to get some." He put one leg up on the barricade before Slocum could grab him. The jerk Slocum gave him was just enough to let the bullet sear his cheek instead of killing him. He tumbled back on top of Slocum. "Beg your pardon, sir," he gasped. In this critical moment all the man could think of was to apologize for falling on top of his captain.

"Hold on, son," Slocum said. "Hold on. Be a soldier. You'll get your water yet."

"Yes, Cap'n," the man said. He was trembling.

"Tonight," Slocum said. "You can hold out till tonight. You can do that much."

"Yes, sir."

"Put a little round pebble in your mouth."

The man scrabbled in the dirt. He was half dazed. The horses, too, were moaning for water.

"Tonight," Slocum said. "Tonight we'll all drink. Keep a sharp lookout, everyone. Get as much rest as you can now."

A wind sprang up and covered everything with a filthy haze. The dust blew upward through the chaparral and turned the sun's savage yellow disc into a bronze gong that struck as viciously as it had been doing all day at the panting, gasping men and horses. Occasionally an Apache barked like a coyote.

The dead horses and men were starting to stink. The men had to lie flat. They had to urinate in that position, right where they were. The ground was saturated with the acrid stench. The sun reached the zenith and began its incredibly slow descent, as if it had to force its way through the sky. At four Horton sent Rigby to summon all those officers who were left alive—a total of four.

Horton's face had been seared by the sun to a dull red. He stared at the ground for a full minute before he spoke. "As you know, we're pretty badly off here." His hands kept squeezing nervously at his knees. His gray stubble had grown longer. His once mirror-perfect boots were badly scratched by the frequent crawling over the rubble-strewn hilltop.

"Pretty badly off," he repeated. The officers were embarrassed and looked at their hands, not wishing to stare at him. He seemed suddenly old and ineffectual.

"Most of the horses are dead. We must get water tonight. The wounded are dying from lack of it. But there's a full moon tonight. They know we'll make a try for the water soon, and they will have the river guarded. There's no way we can make a cavalry charge. Not with the way the ground is broken up by all those goddamn ravines.

"We will have to go by foot. And, if we do, we will have no cover till we manage to drive them out of one of the ravines. Once we do that we'll have another ravine to drive them out of. Our ammunition is very low. We lost over half the ammunition pack mules trying to get up here. But there is nothing else we can do. We must accept our losses. Lieutenant Granger."

"Sir."

"You will make sure your men carry nothing but their carbines, ammunition, and a canteen. Leave the sabers. You will take your—"

"Sir."

"Was that you, Snow? Did you just speak?"

"Yes, sir."

Horton stared at Slocum in hatred. "Don't you know better than to talk to me?" he asked with passion. "The only time I want to hear your voice again is when you give the answers at your court-martial! Now get out!"

Slocum rose. His knowledge that he could scarcely be court-martialed gave him some control, but he had had enough of Horton's abrasive, contemptuous tone.

"Sir. We are short of officers. If you wish, Colonel, I

shall be happy to place myself under arrest as soon as we are off the hill. But until then—''

"Did you hear me?" Horton shouted. Men turned around all through the position and stared. "Do as I say, or—" He unbuttoned the flap of his holster. Rigby dropped his hand to his holster flap. Slocum looked at both of them. He would not stand there patiently and let himself be shot by anyone, and he was ready to start the necessary action.

Horton seemed to sense this. "No," he said thickly. He buttoned the flap. "I'm not your type, Snow. I'll settle this argument traditionally." His voice had dropped to its usual low, controlled tone. "Go to your place in the line and stay there," he finished. Slocum stared at Horton for a few seconds, then turned away. He had not been there five minutes when Lieutenant Granger, a man who kept his counsel to himself in a quiet, competent manner Slocum liked, came over and sat beside him.

"You're next in command, Snow," he remarked.

"What about it?"

"Someone will have to take over soon. He's getting a bit crazy, I think. He said you deliberately shot Palmer in order to help Cummings, who was jealous of the colonel for all his promotions while the captain didn't get any."

"Oh, what crap," Slocum said.

"He's got it all arranged in his head, that it's all part of a scheme to discredit him. He says you deliberately failed to charge the *rancheria* so that the Apaches could push him across the river and pin him up here. He's going to draw up a list of charges as long as your arm so that the trial at Fort Grant will become the most famous court-martial in the history of the army."

"What else?"

"I'm sure he has visions of a heroic charge down the hill with everyone yelling and waving and following his guidon. Holy mackerel, I wouldn't go down there for all the shoulder bars in the army. Would you?"

"No. Not that way."

"So you think we should sit it out?"

"No. No point. By tomorrow we have to have water or we'll be finished."

Granger sighed. "So—" he began. Slocum interrupted him. "Do you know where the pack mule is? The one that carried the signal rockets?"

"I think so. But if you're thinking of signaling for help, you had better lie down till you feel better."

"Was it one of those lost in the river crossing?"

"I don't think so, Captain. But I don't see—"

"*Where is that mule's pack?*"

"I guess somewhere along to the left."

"Get it."

Granger got up, grumbling a little, but he found the pack and brought it back. "What do you—"

"Open it, open it, man!"

A little infected with Slocum's enthusiasm, Granger proceeded to open the pack. It was soaked through from the river. One dozen rockets dripped water.

Granger, seeing Slocum's face, said, "Well, it was a thought."

"Open the bundle."

Granger took out his knife and cut the bundle apart. In the very center were three completely dry rockets.

"With these," Slocum said with a slow grin, "every man and mule and horse in the command will have his belly full of water by dawn tomorrow."

Granger didn't understand.

Slocum stood up. "I'm going to see Horton," he said briefly.

"He won't talk to you. If you could have heard what he said—"

Slocum did not reply. Granger followed him to where the colonel was. He found Horton sitting cross-legged, staring up at the sky, trying to figure out how many hours were left until dawn and his last attack.

"Sir," Slocum began.

"Get out," Horton said with a tired air.

"The Apaches know that rockets are used by commands to signal one another at night," Slocum said. "We have rockets—"

"And signal Fort Grant, eh? Don't be ridiculous, Snow."

But Horton had begun to listen. Slocum pressed the advantage.

"We'll send up a rocket—"

"From *here?* What the hell's the point of that?"

"A *mile* from here. Just before sunrise."

"How will that rocket get there?"

"I'll walk it over."

Horton's face got red. He did not want Slocum out of his sight. He wanted Slocum in excellent condition, alive and well at Fort Grant, in good shape for a court-martial. He did not want him in any situation where he might get himself killed.

"Go on," he said icily. "Go on with this fairy tale."

"When the rocket goes up," Slocum explained patiently, "you'll answer here with another rocket."

"What's the point?"

"They'll think another big attack will be coming from the direction of the first rocket."

Horton looked at him with contempt.

"Suppose," he said, "that their scouts are out covering the country so tightly that they know damn well there isn't a single trooper within a hundred miles?"

"Fair enough," Slocum said. "And I'll tell you what they'll think when they see that signal rocket I'll be sending up. They'll think that the damn fool scout watching the trail went to sleep somewhere instead of watching the trail."

Horton suddenly smiled at the idea. This time it was an

amused smile; he was smiling at the idea of both white and red leaders sharing the same irritated cynicism toward their men.

Slocum sensed what Horton was thinking and pressed his advantage.

"There's no *single* Apache commander," he said. "There's lots of commanders. Lots of little bands together down there. Each of 'em's got a war leader. Each chief has a different way of doing things. They argue, yell, hit one another. Apaches don't do things like white soldiers. They sort of agree to go along on a war party. But if they don't like the way things are going—not enough pickings, too many shot, too many owls heard at night, bad luck signs like that—why, they just pick up and go. And if they don't like taking an order from the war chief, they just don't take it. So, if someone were chosen to watch the trail, and if he doesn't report anything even if a rocket shot up from his position, any war chief would very likely think that he just decided to come back and join the fighting to get himself a carbine from a dead soldier, or get himself a horse, or help cut up a soldier down in that *rancheria*."

Horton was convinced. He weighed the advantage of such a solution to his impossible position up on the hill versus his desire to see that Snow be well protected and survive to face the court-martial he so dearly wanted. After all, he realized, Snow really knew his Apaches and their system of warfare. It was Horton's only chance, and he knew he had better take it.

"So they see the rocket. Then what?" he asked.

"They'll pull off at least half their warriors to deal with the attack they're sure will be coming. Then you'll have a good chance to make a run for it through the half that's left. One more thing. When they think the other command is on its way, even those Apaches left here won't be eager to stay around."

"Why not?" Horton demanded.

"They'll be too anxious to put their women and children in a safe place."

"Well, Snow, there's nothing wrong with that idea except that it's not got a damn thing to do with strategy." Horton paused. "Reason? I don't want to evacuate a position that's impregnable defensively. Is that clear?"

So the man had reversed himself, Slocum thought bitterly.

Horton continued, "I came to Mexico to kill Apaches. And the way to kill them is when they're in front of you and when you're dug in."

"The water—" Slocum began, but Horton cut him off.

"You will note, Snow, that we could climb up and down hills for years and not flush out a dozen redskins. Will you admit that?"

"Yes, sir. Nevertheless—"

Horton held up a hand. "I've got *hundreds* surrounding me in a superb defensive position! Do you understand that? We'll kill more of 'em in three days as soon as they get restless and start charging at us, than in three months of chasing them across their goddamn deserts! We're paying for it, but we can't have victories without taking a few slaps ourselves. They'll get restless down there. They can't endure a siege. They'll need to go hunting for food. They cooperated to get us up here, but that was a miracle. Since everyone commands they'll start to disintegrate soon. They've scared away all the deer with the shooting. They've probably eaten just about all their mesquite beans and mescal roots. Anyone smelled mescal roasting?" He looked around challengingly.

Slocum looked at him with admiration. There was nothing wrong with Horton's thinking; nothing wrong with the way he had appropriated Slocum's knowledge of Apache behavior. But he had forgotten the most essential thing— they were out of water.

"And so," Horton finished, leaning forward and slapping his right hand on his thigh triumphantly, "they'll get disgusted. Know what they'll do then? They'll go wild and charge up the hill at us, and we'll pick 'em off like ripe peaches off a tree!''

He swung his hand in a wide exuberant gesture, knocking down the guidon Rigby had planted beside him. Rigby caught the guidon in a fast grab and reset it.

Slocum had to end this self-delusion. ''Sir, the men are starting to kill the mules and drink their blood. Each charge they make will cost us more men. The Apaches will take losses, but they can lose more than we can.''

Lieutenant Granger said, ''I'm afraid he's right.''

Horton asked, ''You think there's a possibility of mutiny?''

Lieutenant Granger hesitated. The pause was very clear. Horton stared at the ground. His temporary enthusiasm had dissipated.

''Rigby.''

''Sir.''

''You know pretty well how the men feel.''

''Yes, sir.''

''Well?''

Rigby stamped the hard ground more firmly around the guidon shaft, avoiding the colonel's eyes.

''Well—god damn it?''

''Sir, I'll do my duty, sir.''

''I'm not asking you for a patriotic speech, man! Will the men hold for another day or two?''

Rigby turned a deep red. He spoke, barely audibly. ''They have to have water, sir.''

Another thump of bowstrings came from the ravine. One arrow struck a picketed horse. In its frantic, agonized plunging the horse kicked a wounded man in his ribs. The man screamed.

''Shoot that goddamn horse!'' Horton yelled. His voice was close to hysteria.

A sergeant fired. At the sound of the shot several Apaches

laughed. One shouted, "How, how, how! How do you do, white soldiers? Listen!"

Silence fell on the hilltop. Then came the sound of water splashing into a tin basin.

"You come over," said the same voice. "We *amigos*. You come over with your carbine and ammunition. We give you plenny water. We no touch you. We see you get to Messican town. We give you back horses you lose in river! And plenny, *plenny* water!"

"All right, Snow," Horton said. His voice was tired. "What's your plan with the rockets?"

14

"I'll set it off across the river on the *rancheria* side," Slocum began. "As soon as it goes up, everyone here will yell things like, 'There they are at last!' 'There's the good old Third Cavalry!' 'What took the Third so long to get here?' And so forth." He grinned.

"Then," he went on, "since they must have a good translator with them, I know I can rely on him to spread the word. Give 'em ten minutes to talk it over while everyone up here makes plenty of noise to welcome the Third.

"I'll send up the second rocket much closer. That should do it: they'll rush down the hill and across the river to protect the women and children. They'll leave just a few men here for a holding force, if anyone will be willing to stay behind while his family is supposedly in danger. About five minutes after the second rocket, make your charge on a narrow front. Punch through to the river, get a good drink, and then charge the *rancheria*. They'll pull out fast, convinced that there *is* a Third Cavalry. You can hold a good piece of the riverfront while you fill your canteens and round up as many of our horses as you can."

"All right. Volunteers?"

"With all due respect, sir," Granger said, "the only

man who can get through will have to speak Apache.
Captain Snow is the only one I know who can.''

Horton lifted a hand, made a fist, and drove it, clenched,
against his thigh. Slocum knew the sign of a man backed
to the wall. Horton wanted Snow alive for a court-martial,
but the only way he could have a live Snow for that—and
have a command left alive—was for Snow to risk his life
in disguise. And one more thing that Horton was sweating
out: if Snow survived, he could very well receive a citation
for his heroism. And if that happened, if Horton could not
block it, then Snow might very well be let off lightly at the
court-martial.

''All right,'' Horton said thickly. There would be no
concealing any of the incidents of that day; nothing could
be glossed over in his reports when they returned to Fort
Grant. Too many rank and file would be questioned, and
too many of them hated him by now.

Slocum squatted in a tiny hollow and, over a small fire,
trimmed as much beard as he could with the doctor's
scissors. He had to look as clean-shaven as possible. Apaches
never had facial hair. He filled a coffee mug with mule
blood, sifted some dirt into it, and stirred it with a forefinger.
He stripped naked and rubbed the mixture over his legs
and body till he looked dark enough to pass muster. Since
he would be facing plenty of Apaches on his way down the
hill, he would have to do better in the matter of hair. He
cut off several bunches of horsehair from the tails of dead
horses. Draping them over his head, he tied them in place
with a headband made from his neckerchief. It would do.
He put on the breechclout he had worn coming up the hill,
and the knee-high moccasins.

He crossed two bandoliers over his chest in the Apache
style. Around his waist he buckled a gun belt with his own
Colt. He slid a knife into the belt. He looked like a very
successful Apache warrior; a close examination would have

revealed his green eyes, but even that discovery would not have been fatal. Many people living as Apaches had been taken as children from Mexican or American families. Still, Slocum did not intend to stand by patiently for any detailed examinations.

He carefully stowed two rockets inside the dirty white blouse he had worn coming up the hill. He looked around and saw Lieutenant Granger. Slocum decided that the young lieutenant possessed the necessary qualities of intelligence and sharpness he needed. He handed the third rocket to Granger.

"As soon as mine goes up, send yours up. Got some dry matches?"

Granger swallowed. "Yes."

"Keep the rocket dry, Granger."

Horton was again sitting cross-legged on his blanket. He stared at Slocum and said nothing as he watched Slocum stand up while the full moon finally sank behind the ridge. He nodded to Granger, who ordered the third squad to fire and create a diversion at the other end of the lines. The flashes and roars of the carbines were enough distraction for Slocum to slide over the barricade and writhe forward. He hoped the racket would be enough to attract the Apaches' attention.

Slocum reached a flat slab of loose gray shale without any problems. The shale still held some of the heat of the day. Very slowly, lest he make a noise in dislodging any loose rock, he placed one hand after the other and tested for a piece that might rattle and betray him when his weight would be placed on it. After he had moved thirty feet his bare knees began to bleed.

The firing stopped. Slocum cursed silently. Granger had promised to keep them busy at it till he himself gave the next signal. When he reached the end of the shale he put his left hand down directly onto a rattlesnake.

He knew what that cold, smooth mass was as soon as he

touched it, but he was not fast enough to get out of the way of its strike. He felt a jar as the fangs struck the bandolier. They made a little sharp tinkling sound. It took the greatest effort for Slocum not to yell or roll to one side to avoid a second strike.

He froze. The rattler uncoiled and flowed away, furious at being disturbed from its warm resting place.

Slocum stayed motionless. He was less than fifty feet from the nearest ravine, and he prayed that the small happening had passed unnoticed. He hoped that Granger would be ready to carry out his own chore as soon as Slocum gave the signal in a minute or so. His naked chest felt wet. For one terrible moment he thought that the snake's fangs had penetrated his skin. But when he tested the temperature of the fluid it was chilly: venom. He put his hand carefully on the shale and felt two small curved pieces of material that resembled ivory in their smoothness. The two broken-off fangs. No problem for the snake; it would just go hungry till it grew two new ones. Slocum let out a deep, relieved breath.

He crawled infinitely slowly. He hoped that the snake would have sense enough to get off the shale and go to ground somewhere. Slocum doubted his ability to remain silent if the goddamn rattler would strike again.

When he was twenty-five feet from the ravine he leaped to his feet, threw a rock at the barricade and yelled, "How, how, how, pony soldiers!"

Several carbines crashed on the hill, all aimed at him.

Only the soldiers on the hill knew that the bullets had first been extracted from the cartridges. Slocum threw himself flat, got up, and ran to the ravine. Convinced that Slocum was an Apache, the other Apaches moved aside to permit him to dive headlong over the ravine edge as another blank volley crashed out.

Slocum slid down the side of the ravine in a shower of dust and small stones. He knocked someone over as he was halfway down. The man got up angrily and pushed Slocum aside.

"Brother!" Slocum said sarcastically in Apache.

Several Apaches laughed. Slocum turned and picked his way slowly along the bottom of the ravine. It was packed with men and horses. They were trying to get back to sleep after the sudden burst of firing. Little cooking fires burned everywhere. There seemed to be a heavy traffic of horses being walked down the ravine and to the river, and other horses being led uphill again. It was clear that the ones coming up had been taken down to be watered and fed in the lush grass along the river bottom. Slocum kept his distance from the fires. All the Apaches were heavily armed. Some carried two carbines; others had as many as three revolvers stuck in their belts. Some were carefully counting out piles of ammunition and placing it in U.S. Cavalry saddlebags.

Up and down the ravine floor were bunches of arrows that had been driven into the ground. Groups of women were making fire arrows out of them and setting the completed ones to one side.

Slocum continued with his descent. An Apache with two carbines looked up at Slocum. "Hello," he said, "I will trade you one for your revolver."

Slocum shook his head and kept going. He wove in and out between the horses. Further down two Apaches were sitting on a log eating jerky. One of them wore a fine custom-made pair of boots. They looked like Cummings's. The other Apache wore a vest that had been looted from a rancher's home. The usual bandoliers were slung across it. In one of the vest pockets was a gold watch. As Slocum passed the man pulled out the watch and wound it ostentatiously with a gold key. Then he held it to an ear and enjoyed its ticking. His eyes widened when he saw Slocum's gun. It was a very good one and had an ivory butt.

He stood up and pulled out the watch. "It is magic," he

told Slocum, who had stopped reluctantly. To keep moving might have aroused suspicion. "The important white men always carry one like it. I like your gun."

Slocum shook his head. The Apache squeezed his thumb and the case flew open. "See?" he said proudly.

Slocum shook his head and turned away. The Apache followed him. "I *like* your gun," he repeated.

Slocum moved away, still shaking his head. The man was unusually stubborn. He had gone past the bounds of good Apache manners. He had been drinking some captured whiskey. His gait was not very steady. The man stepped closer and held the watch to Slocum's ear. If he had been sober he would have noticed something unusual about the way Slocum's hair was sitting on his head, but he was too interested in the gun.

Some other Apaches were chuckling at the man's insistence. The warrior shifted the watch to Slocum's other ear. Sooner or later—and probably sooner—he would dislodge the wig, and there would be a sudden, violent end to it all.

Afraid that the wig might be dislodged with the man's clumsy insistence, Slocum took the watch and pretended to listen to it while he examined the man's throat and chest.

The crossed bandoliers protected the heart. He wore three heavy silver and turquoise necklaces which effectively kept his throat safe from a quick knife slash across the jugular. Slocum made his choice.

No one was looking at them. Slocum handed over his gun. The man took it and gave the watch to Slocum. The Apache turned away and Slocum, relieved, was prepared to let him go, when the man suddenly spun around and grabbed Slocum by the arm.

"Come and drink *tiswin* with me!" he shouted. *Tiswin* was a fermented drink. Slocum pulled his elbow away and shook his head. The Apache reached out once more for

Slocum's shoulder, and this time he grabbed a bunch of horsehair. He pulled and Slocum's disguise came off. ·

Slocum acted fast. He grabbed the man's elbow and pulled hard. The man spun and presented his back to Slocum. He raised his head to shout a warning to the others, but Slocum flung a muscular forearm around his neck and took a long step backward so that the Apache's heels were on the ground. Off balance he could do nothing except try to pry away the arm that was tightening at his throat. He might have been able to do it with his great strength in a few seconds, but Slocum had pulled the knife from his belt. It went in to the hilt in the man's neck.

He gave a sudden convulsive shudder, jerked twice, and then sagged in Slocum's grip. This all took place in absolute quiet. Slocum held the man until he was sure that he was dead. He dragged him to the river, took his gun back, let the body sink into the water, then shoved it gently out into the current.

He knelt down and took a long drink. He met no one as he moved along the riverbank. When he came opposite the *rancheria* he wove in and out between several dark mounds: the dead horses and mules that had been killed when the platoon had made a last desperate stand. Scattered between the dead animals were the stripped and mutilated bodies of the men who had fought behind them until they were overrun after their ammunition gave out. Mingled among the corpses were empty cartridge cases shining faintly in the moonlight, along with loose letters and emptied wallets. Paper money rustled in the wind and blew in the branches of the scrub willows.

Across the river the Apaches lay sleeping in their *jacales*. As the dogs picked up Slocum's scent they began their frantic barking, but no one paid any attention.

An hour later Slocum was a mile up the river and sitting on a ridge top. The climb had been hard up the steep slope. The watch ticked gently away. A pink glow appeared in the east. He laid the rocket against a sloping rock, placed a flat rock underneath for a base, and set several small rocks around the rocket shaft for a guide.

Then he lit the fuse.

The rocket soared up and up. Then it burst overhead, lighting up the top of the hill with its green glare. The explosion could be heard for miles. A shower of small, sizzling green balls rained down.

Four seconds later the rocket back on the hilltop where the remnant of the command lay went up in answer. Even Slocum, standing a mile and a half away, could see the tiny green balls falling down with slow delicacy.

Now there was light enough for Slocum to see what was happening in the *rancheria* across the river. Tiny figures were beginning to run around there like ants in a disturbed anthill.

Slocum began to run along the ridge toward the command, forcing himself through the thickets. He found a bear trail and followed that. The Apaches believed that bears were great travelers and always took the easiest way.

Sharp stones pressed into his thin moccasin soles. Although he had pulled the long Apache moccasins up to his knees, his bare thighs were badly scratched.

He scrambled over boulders instead of going around them. He forced his way through a heavy stand of scrub pine after the bear trail headed downhill toward the water. He needed a prominent summit. He finally burst out on the summit, panting and sweating.

Quickly he made another base from scattered rocks. He set the rocket down gently inside and lit it. It went straight up and burst directly overhead with a sound like a thunderclap.

When the first rocket burst those few Apaches who were awake and looking in that direction believed that a god had spoken. One or two of the more sophisticated thought it was an artillery piece, but they were as terrified as the others. It was an amazing feat to have transported a field gun into those mountains, and any troops who could do that were undefeatable.

All the others woke at the sound of the explosion. They crawled swiftly through the low doors of their *jacales*. By the time Granger sent up his rocket in answer most of the Apaches in the *rancheria* saw it, as well as those who had been sleeping in the ravines waiting for dawn and the last desperate charge of the command for water.

If the Apaches were to withdraw to defend their women and children against the new attack that they were sure would be following soon upon the rockets, they knew that the soldiers would outflank them with a dearly won knowledge of the terrain.

This time there would no luring the soldiers into a trap.

The strategic reasons reinforced the supernatural ones. The best thing to do, as far as they were concerned, would be to pull out quickly and entirely from this accessible valley, then climb to where no white soldier could follow on a horse.

By the time the command had entered the *rancheria,* all the Apaches had fled high up, where only a sure-footed mountain goat could follow. To pursue them there with Horton's depleted command would be sheer suicide.

Only one white prisoner was still alive. He had been stripped naked except for his boots, which were just too large for the smaller Apaches to wear, so he had been allowed to keep them. His face had been sliced away with sharp knives till he was unrecognizable.

Horton bent over him. The man opened his eyes and tried to talk, but he could not form any words without lips. The words made no sense. Horton bent lower, but the man could only blow a froth of blood into the colonel's face.

There was no way the remnant of the command could go after the Apaches. They had retreated through a narrow

arroyo, and the rimrock overhead was lined with huge
boulders. As Horton watched he could see the black heads
of the Apache rear guard flitting from rock to rock. They
were preparing to dislodge the boulders should there be
any pursuit along the arroyo.

On the far side was a desert ninety miles across. Horton
was checkmated. He smashed his fist against the pommel.
His blouse was wet from the blood of the tortured trooper.
Rigby watched him and felt like crying in shame.

After Slocum had set off the second rocket he squatted on
his heels and waited. In full daylight the crude wig would
fool no one. He pulled it off and threw it away.

From his high position he could see everything below
him clearly, as if it were a three-dimensional map on
which the cartographer had scattered mountains, rivers,
toy soldiers, and toy Indians.

The toy Indians were running along the unexpected
ravines that had been the death trap for the command,
riding toy horses and kicking up dust clouds. After a while
smoke began to pour out of the *jacales*. The Apaches were
setting fire to them to prevent anything useful falling into
the hands of the soldiers—blankets, bedding, clothes, food.
They would be able to carry none of these things with
them in their frantic flight. The soldiers in blue began to
move down the hill and file along the ravines. The Indians
were retreating before them.

At the river the soldiers and horses stopped. Slocum
shrugged. It was important for Horton to pursue and destroy,
but no force in the world could have stopped the men from
moving on until they drank their fill. Slocum didn't give a
damn, anyway. It was not his fight; no medals or promotions awaited him.

He stood up and slid down a ravine bank in a shower of
dust and pebbles. He heard voices suddenly, and the sound
of unshod horses moving closer. He slipped behind a rock

and waited till the Apaches went by. One wore a lieutenant's blue coat that had two bloody holes over the heart. Behind him sat a small girl. She clung to his waist. In her left hand she clutched a pack of dirty, greasy playing cards that had belonged to a trooper who had been cut off at the river.

Then followed three women. Each rode bareback on a horse with US branded on its flank. Each horse carried several US saddlebags slung across it. In the overstuffed bags Slocum could see blue pants and boots. The Apaches were excited and spoke quickly and quietly. From time to time they looked over their shoulders for signs of pursuit.

Half an hour passed. No one else had come by. Slocum kneeled and pressed an ear to the ground. He could not hear any sound of hooves coming nearer. He decided he would do better to move just below the ridge, popping up occasionally for a quick look at the trail. As he climbed he began to feel thirsty again. It was time to get down to the river, drink his fill, find an abandoned canteen, fill it, and then keep moving. He had signed off from the United States Cavalry; it was time to get back to the States and look around for something profitable, interesting, and, he hoped, less dangerous than this Indian-chasing business.

As he patrolled in and out of the sagebrush and cactus, Rigby, two hundred yards away on the next ridge, put down a pair of field glasses and grinned savagely. If there was no way to bring back Captain Snow for a court-martial, then Rigby had decided he would have his own court-martial right there.

He picked up the sniper's Springfield that was lying beside him.

Rigby was a superb shot. He lined up Snow's head in the V-shaped notch. Since the captain was moving toward him there was no need to lead. Rigby had placed the barrel on his folded jacket. It would absorb the shock of the explosion nicely. Rigby squeezed the trigger gently till he had taken up the slack. The captain's head was dead center. Rigby squeezed and the heavy gun jumped.

15

What saved Slocum's life, and what made him ever afterwards reluctant to kill rattlesnakes, was the fact that a rattlesnake suddenly slid out in front of him. It coiled, its massive arrow-shaped head swaying as its tongue took messages from the air.

A minute fraction of a second after Slocum stepped backwards, the firing pin of the Springfield struck the cartridge. Rigby was not to be blamed if he thought that Captain Snow had been hit in the head; but what Slocum's slight move accomplished was to ensure that the heavy bullet seared the side of his head instead of blowing it apart like a ripe melon.

The great cliff in back of him bellowed. He twisted to the left and fell. Half dazed, temporarily paralyzed with the shock, he knew it would be best not to move until his head cleared.

Rigby rose with a tight grin and ejected the spent cartridge, heedlessly exposing himself to any Apache who might be near. It was such a moment of triumph that he didn't care.

"And how do you like that, Captain Snow?" he whispered. He raised the Springfield aloft and shook it exultantly.

* * *

"Lieutenant Granger."

"Sir."

Horton halted. The command had watered and filled their canteens. They found plenty of ammunition in the abandoned *rancheria,* along with enough jerky salvaged from the fires to take care of their food wants on the march back. They buried the dead and walked their horses back and forth over the graves so as to make sure that the bodies could not be dug up and further mutilated should the Apaches return.

"Lieutenant, I'm promoting you to captain. You will take over Captain Cummings's and Captain Snow's responsibilities."

"Yes, sir!"

"Permit no stragglers—can't abide 'em. You see what happens to anyone who's taken prisoner by these red bastards. Pick a couple of good men and have 'em scout ahead."

"Yes, sir. Can I take a couple of men and look for Captain Snow?"

"What the hell for? The man's a deserter!"

"Sir, I beg to differ. He could be hiding out till the Apaches clear out. They're all over the hills waiting for stragglers—"

"I don't want you roaming around out there and getting yourself and your men ambushed!" Horton shouted.

"Sir—"

"You've got a long way to go in this army, Granger." Horton gritted his teeth, barely able to control himself. "Don't make it hard for yourself."

Granger reddened and stared at the ground.

Horton expelled a long breath. He had taken control of himself. "Granger," he said softly, "I know how you feel. You liked Snow. I can understand that. He took you under his wing and gave you a course on the Sierra Madre. It's natural to feel grateful to the man, but the overall interests of the Army are what counts. He didn't want to face a court-martial, so he deserted.'' Horton's voice grew stronger. "And I don't want to risk a single trooper's life on a wild-goose chase. Dismissed.''

Slocum was unconscious. He saw a horseman riding by, leaning on his pommel. Blood was pouring from his mouth. It was Henderson, who had died at White Oak Swamp. He said, "Hallo, Slocum! Thirsty?'' He paid no attention to the great gouts of blood pulsing from his mouth, but lifted his canteen and held it out invitingly.

Slocum reached out. Henderson said in a teasing way, "Remember Savage's farmhouse? On the Staunton Pike? Brandy from his cellar!'' Slocum held out his hand. Henderson tilted the canteen and poured it out on the ground. It was not brandy, but blood. Henderson chuckled and rode on, chanting, "*Bueno, bueno!*''

Then Wilson rode by, very yellow and prosaic, reading a map through his old-fashioned spectacles; then came Roberts, lithe, cheerful and whistling; and gray sinister Darcy; and white-bearded insane Winter. Squads of saber men followed, driving barefooted prisoners to and fro like cattle.

Then someone seemed to be sawing out a section of Slocum's skull. He dreamed of baked ham stuck all over with fragrant cloves. The cloves became fangs, and came closer and closer. Slocum started to yell and choked.

He woke up sweating. For a second he didn't know where he was. Then he remembered. The shot had come from the troopers. And the only man there who qualified as a sharpshooter was Rigby.

He placed a dirty palm against his throbbing head. They were several hours ahead of him on horseback, and he was afoot. It might be a good idea to catch up with them and settle this with Rigby.

He prowled through the abandoned *rancheria* and assem-

bled enough clothes to dress as a soldier. He even managed to find a pair of boots that fit him. There were no
horses. Grimly, he began to follow the command's trail to
the north.

The hot plain was sluggish and inert. It was filled with
greasewood and salt bushes.

Dull white stretches of blinding white alkali ran aimlessly through the brown bushes. Heat blurred the edges of
everything. Once the heat haze shifted and lifted lazily for
a brief moment. He saw a small round lake misted over
with its own steam. The bitter water was poisonous. Then
the haze shook down again and the lake disappeared.

Across his body was slung the most important thing in
the world—his canteen. He never drank. He sipped, and
rinsed the warm, flat liquid around until it moistened the
lining of his mouth. Then he let it trickle back into the
canteen. From time to time a lizard's tail would slide
deeper into its hole or a hairy-backed tarantula would
scuttle across in front of him.

Everywhere there was silence. There was no sound of
the wind blowing, no bird calls, no insects chirping.
It seemed to Slocum after a while that he was on a
treadmill, with the desert going backward under him. The
only way to keep sane in this terrifying sameness was to
pick out a landmark and aim at it. When it was reached,
then he would pick out something else distinctive: a mis-
shapen Joshua tree or a clump of sagebrush. Then he
would walk toward that. When it was reached he would
repeat the process. It gave him the illusion that he was
moving.

Sweat soaked through his blue cavalry trousers. His
hands became puffed up from the cactus needles that
were impossible to avoid whenever he passed jumping
cholla.

Toward late afternoon of the following day he came to a

river that was only a few feet wide. It was filled brim to brim with brown water due to a cloudburst far to the west in the mountains. As he bellied down on the bank he stopped. Bones of rabbits and birds littered the banks. They had drunk the water which had become poisonous in its race over the alkali flats.

Later that day, the land began to rise and he began to see scattered live oaks. His canteen held only a mouthful. He did not know if he could hold out any longer. His feet felt like lead. It was painful walking in his boots, but he knew that if he took them off he wouldn't be able to get them on again. He rounded a slope and a tiny current of air flowed past him, cooling his cheeks.

He knew then that he was in the foothills, and in the distance he saw a large cloud of dust moving slowly at a right angle to his course.

The command.

16

The cool, acrid scent of crunched ferns drifted up as Slocum lay on his belly. He plunged his head deep into the cold water and opened his eyes. Round white pebbles shone at the bottom like huge pearls in the shadow of the pine trees that fringed the pool. With his head still underneath, he heard the small waterfall plunging into the other end of the pool.

He pulled out his dripping head. Something nagged at his consciousness. Slocum always paid attention to information coming in that had not yet reached his level of awareness. He tried to pin it down. Then he knew.

The faintest hint of blue was drifting across the sky. Someone had heard him coming and had put out a very small fire. In these mountains the only people who made very small fires were Apaches.

A flock of tiny wild birds flew overhead. Their long, iridescent tail feathers streamed behind them. They settled down in a tree just above Slocum and beat at each other with their wings. They hung upside down from the branches, squawking and quarrelling as they fought for the brilliant orange berries.

They noticed Slocum and suddenly became quiet. He was moving toward the smoke over the pine needles. He made no sound, but the birds kept him company, flapping from tree to tree. Slocum, half amused, half angry, shook his carbine at them. They hopped down to the lowest branches and examined him with fascinated squawks. There was no way Slocum could continue to move unobserved. He paused, debating what to do next.

Something was moving in the tall ferns. It was wrinkled and gray. Very slowly Slocum brought the carbine around to bear. A dry pine twig cracked among the fern fronds.

A very old Apache slowly arose. One eye had been blasted out long ago by a heavy bullet. The other one was clouded over with a milky white substance.

He was barefoot. Aside from a filthy breechclout he wore nothing else. His yellow toenails were long and twisted. In one hand he held an old bow; in his other trembling hand he held a blunt-tipped hunting arrow used for birds.

Slocum lowered the carbine. The man must have been over ninety years old, Slocum judged. The old man began to turn, bent over in a crouch. His long gray hair fell forward over his shoulders.

"*U-ka-she!*" the old man said. "Get away!"

In the tall ferns the eyes of his old squaw shone like a rabbit's. The old man began whining in a dull monotone.

The old man continued to whine. He fitted the hunting arrow to the bow with shaking hands. Slocum suddenly realized that the old, emaciated warrior was singing his death song.

Slocum could just about have encircled the old man's upper arm with his thumb and forefinger. The old Apache was starving. He started to draw back the bowstring. Then he looked surprised and bent his head to listen.

Slocum heard it at the same time. The advance patrol was coming up. What the hell, Slocum thought; they had enough food to spare it for the two old people. If they didn't get it today they'd be dead by morning.

The old man looked anxiously toward the trail. Slowly his trembling arms lowered the bow.

"Wait," Slocum said in Apache. "I will get you food."

" 'baccy?"

"Tobacco too."

Warily the old man withdrew into the ferns and waited.

The advance, carbines across the pommels of their saddles, rode into sight. They reined, prepared to fire, but stopped in amazement when they saw Slocum.

"I'll be goddamned," the corporal who was commanding the patrol said. He rose partly up in his stirrups and looked over his shoulder.

In a moment Horton rode around the bend in the trail. Four paces to his rear rode Rigby, with the colonel's guidon in his stirrup.

Horton stopped short. Slocum had never seen such naked, uncontrolled hatred on a man's face in his life. With a great effort, Horton seized control of himself. He lifted a hand and the command came to a halt behind him.

"Ah, Snow," he said. "Glad you joined us. Fifteen minutes."

The command dismounted wearily. All along the line they stretched in the coolness.

"I'll drop the desertion charge, Snow," he said, with a grim smile. "I'll still deal with you for cowardice, insubordination, and murder. You are under arrest."

Slocum stared at him. For a while he had thought that the complete washout of the man's strategy had humbled him somewhat, but he was wrong.

"Anything to say?" the colonel snapped.

"Nope," Slocum said.

Horton's face turned fiery red. "I'll try you here, right now, you son of a bitch! And if I want to, I'll hang you from the tree you're under! What do you say to that, eh?"

"I'll tell you," Slocum said gently. "You're insane."

"Give me your gun!"

Slocum's eyes shifted to Rigby. The orderly had unbuttoned his holster flap in what he thought was an unobtrusive manner, but Slocum's eyes had caught it immediately. Rigby had also stared at the bullet sear alongside Slocum's head with such intense interest and disappointment that Slocum had no doubt whatsoever that it was Rigby who had shot him.

"I'll not have a dangerous man like you with a gun on him, or running around loose. Granger, get some rope and tie this bastard up. By God, Snow, I'll bring you back to Fort Grant like the murderer you are! Rigby, take his gun!"

Rigby smiled and pulled his gun. As it cleared the holster Slocum kicked hard. The point of his boot caught Rigby's wrist and the gun sailed end over end into the thick stand of ferns.

The ferns crackled. Horton swiftly pivoted his carbine around and saw the old Apache warrior straightening up. In his left hand the old man still held his bow and hunting arrow. His right hand was stretched out toward Horton, palm upwards.

"*Mi amigo!*" he said. " 'baccy?"

Horton fired so swiftly that the old man was still pronouncing his version of "tobacco" when the heavy slug caught him in his thin chest and spun him to the right. Horton pumped once more and fired again. The second bullet caught the old man below his right nipple and knocked him backward into the ferns with his left hand doubled underneath. The third bullet hit him in his shriveled stomach.

Slocum's hand went to his gun butt. Horton had fired his carbine quickly and expertly. Slocum was on fire with the most savage rage he had ever felt in all his years on the frontier.

From deep in the ferns a gun exploded.

Horton's eyes widened in disbelief. He looked down at

his chest. Over his heart a red blot suddenly appeared, as if by magic. As he stared at it, it spread swiftly across his blue coat. His amazed eyes shifted to the ferns.

The old squaw was on her knees. In both her hands she held Rigby's Colt. One finger was missing from her right hand. She slowly lowered the gun. Her hands were too weak to hold it. They trembled with weakness as she lowered it.

"No," Horton said. He shook his head. "No," he said again, as if arguing with a stubborn friend. A spasm of agony twisted his mouth. He toppled from his saddle. As he fell, his head struck the staff of the guidon, and he lay crumpled at the bottom.

Rigby was paralyzed with shock, but he turned and grabbed his carbine from the saddle scabbard. Slocum knocked it out of his hands. Rigby paid no attention to him. He tried to bypass Slocum, screaming, "Lemme get that squaw!"

Slocum slammed the carbine butt brutally against the man's head. The man went down, unconscious. Both he and Horton now lay on the trail.

A breeze sprang up. The little forked flag began to flutter.

"Well, look at that," Slocum said dryly. "Very symbolic, Granger."

"Jesus," Granger said.

"You're in command, Granger," Slocum said. "Take over."

"No—you're in command. You're higher in rank, Captain."

"Nope," Slocum said, grinning. "I'm deserting. As of now."

Granger stared at him openmouthed.

"I've had enough of the cavalry," Slocum said. He mounted Horton's horse.

"But—" Granger began.

"Don't worry about it," Slocum said. "Bury him nice."

He turned and looked at Horton, whose body sprawled across the trail. He looked as if he were asleep.

"He's like the rocket I fired," Slocum said thoughtfully. "It went up and everyone saw how beautiful it was. But no one ever sees where the burnt-out stick comes down. Except us, Granger. We saw it." Slocum took a long breath. "Bury him in the trail and run your horses back and forth over the grave. Wipe out all traces, or they'll come and mutilate him. Good luck, Granger."

Slocum watched. When they had done with Horton they mounted. Rigby's eyes were swollen with weeping. Slocum felt only pity for him now.

He waited until they had all trotted by. Then he turned his horse off the trail and climbed westward, heading somewhere in Sonora where he had never been.